THE STETS

Betty Womack

EROTIC ROMANCE

Siren Publishing, Inc.
www.SirenPublishing.com

A SIREN PUBLISHING BOOK
IMPRINT: Erotic Romance

THE STETSON
Copyright © 2008 by Betty Womack

ISBN: 1-60601-111-1
ISBN: 978-1-60601-111-9

First Publication: December 2008

Cover design by Jinger Heaston
All cover art and logo copyright © 2008 by Siren Publishing, Inc.

Printed in the U.S.A.

PUBLISHER
Siren Publishing, Inc.
www.SirenPublishing.com

DEDICATION

To the cowboy in my life, my husband.

THE STETSON

Betty Womack
Copyright © 2008

Chapter 1

Stranded in a Spartan women's only lodge in Lone Horse Colorado, Abigail knew she had to be careful. A woman on the run couldn't afford to draw attention.

That may have sounded mysterious to someone not in her shoes. Nothing mysterious about escaping the wrath of a grandfather bent on arranging a marriage for you..

Until now, she'd known nothing but a life of ease, the best clothing and education, but her allowance was doled out by the month. If she squandered it quickly, no more was available until the next month.

In hindsight, Abigail regretted her own careless way with money. If she'd only been a little thrifty, she'd be in England, not stuck out here in bear country, waiting for her friend Shane to send money.

Her plans to escape her grandfather's outlandish control didn't become serious until he'd brought home a prospective husband for her. He was the first of many.

The long hours of joy shopping and partying with friends had came home to haunt her. She'd gone from being the girl with bottomless pockets to a virtual bag lady overnight. If Shane didn't get airfare here soon, the interpreter job waiting for her in London would be withdrawn.

Once she got to Puerto Vallarta, her grandmother would help her.

None of this reminiscing did any good now. Morosely, she turned to look down the dusty road.

She used her sleeve to wipe grime from her sunburned forehead, locating the ranch owner, Turk Gunnison.

He stood out like a dark sentinel in the group of riders plodding slowly along the trail. Thank heavens he'd missed her embarrassing and painful tumble and wasn't racing back to explain the rules against straggling behind.

She wanted to cry. What was she doing at this abomination of a resort? That was a joke. This was hell, complete with moose, and she'd just caught sight of a coyote slinking along the shadowed trail just off the road.

This shouldn't be happening to her. She'd worked hard to get her degree in the Language Arts and landed a great job on her own. She should be able to relax at her Grandmother's villa in Puerto Valletta before heading off to England. Not smelling horse dung and dodging Turk Gunnison.

So much for thinking the resident cowboy had missed her accident. He was on his way back to check on her, pinning her with a furious stare.

She groaned with helpless irritation. In desperate times, one tried to strike a deal with the person in charge. Turk was that person. That wouldn't be easy.

If you have any idea of using him, forget it. You have only one thing he might be interested in.

Caught staring at her, he didn't turn his gaze away, that turquoise gaze telling her he knew how she tasted. All the while he was quick to let her know he was keeping her under surveillance because she was a troublemaker.

Lunacy. Thinking about seducing the rough neck while the blasted horse's watched.

Horses, everywhere she looked. Horses cropping at the thick roadside grass, and now the mare she'd been thrown from, munched placidly on the hem of her dirty long sleeved shirt.

"Huffy! That wouldn't have happened if you'd ease up on the reins."

Abigail dusted the seat of her pants and grabbed the reins that dragged on the ground. "I needed to rest my legs."

Why did she nearly explode with a silly mixture of shyness and desire to flirt with the disgusting lodge owner. He was a man that probably preferred his women with manure on their boots.

His knowing stare screamed his growing impatience at her horseman ship. It was plain by his reaction to her constant blunders with the horse's he rated her last in the group of women.

However, the glimmer of male interest in his eyes said something vastly different. He enjoyed looking at her.

He leaned on the saddle horn and smiled languidly down at her. "Is that what you were doing?"

"That's what I said." She swiped at her flyaway hair. "You didn't have to come stampeding back here. I'm fine."

From atop his annoyingly superior position, Turk Gunnison circled around, looking her over with the air of a sultan.

"Who taught you to ride, Huffy?" He held up his left hand to remind her of the proper mounting procedure. "Left to get on, right to get thrown." He laughed, flicking the reins in her direction. "You okay?"

Abigail was in no mood for more biting humor. Especially not by Turk Gunnison. She hated him and his faded Levi's that spotlighted his ample plumbing. Now he pretended to be concerned with her well-being. His ploy may have been more convincing if that damn twinkle hadn't been in his eyes. "I said I am okay. You don't need to stay here."

Criticism coming from him was especially hard to take. She wasn't sure why he struck fire off her. But, God help her, she couldn't help noticing him, the way his grin twisted his mouth into sexy, almost devious invitation. Abigail didn't want to see him as anything more than a jerk in a Stetson.

"You gonna make it?" He did that thing men do astride a horse, lifted his rear up and out of the saddle as if to tell her he was too well packed to sit on it all day. It was intriguing, but she maintained a poker face. He didn't need to know she was attracted to anything about him. "Just wanted to make sure you're all right, Huffy?"

That had sounded sincere.

Don't be fooled by that good looking face, sister. He's up to something.

"That's Ms. Van Huffington to you, cowboy."

He touched the brim of his weathered hat and nodded. "I can see you're fine." By design or not, his gaze dropped to her breast like a shot. "Huffy."

A trickle of excitement spread up from her toes to sizzle around inside her lacy bra, like invisible fingers. His fingers. Untangling her tongue took some time. Ignoring his simmering sensuality was even harder.

"You're not much of a riding teacher. I could have been trampled."

Now she'd done it. He dismounted and walked toward her.

"Not likely, Ms.Huff...Huffy. Maude here..." he stroked the mare's neck. "She's like a baby." He caught Abigail's arm to pull her closer to the beast. "You can be a quitter or face your fear."

Of all the damn places Colorado, why had Shane chosen this one? A place so remote mail was only delivered twice a week. Cedar Mountain Ranch had seemed perfect, until she met whom she'd taken for just another ranch hand.

Her secrets may as well have been written on her face while he eyed her with withering speculation.

The situation became crystal clear. The intimidating cowboy who, like it or not, was in control of her life for the moment.

Okay, so be it. Nothing would be too great a sacrifice to gain her freedom.

Thinking back on their first meeting, he'd been no less than a gentleman, but his brusque manner spoke clearly of his dislike for her. Her plan to complain about him to the owner was dashed on the rocks soon enough.

He was the owner, manager and all things in between. There was no one over him. The two housekeepers spoke little English. The cook, with the original name Cookie, adored him, so there was no use trying to dish the dirt with her.

They smiled and nodded sympathetically each time she poured out her resentment about their boss. She grew more frustrated as she realized he maintained complete control of her.

Scorching heat slipped over her face as she lifted her foot into the stirrup. Damn it. Being a full inch too short to mount with any kind of grace, she hopped on one foot while trying to drag herself onto the horse's back.

His drawl sickened her. "Miss Huffy. I'll be happy to give you a leg up."

She jumped with a start when his hand clamped around her waist. In her fluster, she lost her grip on the saddle horn, sliding down to be caught in his strong hands. Of course, her rear fit perfectly in his broad palms. He didn't give her time to enjoy it, but tossed her up onto the mare's back, resting his hand on her knee while cupping her fingers around the soft leather reins.

"There you go." He inclined his head toward a petite woman that appeared to be in her late sixties astride a huge black gelding and chided Abigail mildly. "Just do whatever Bertha does. This is her first trail ride too, but she follows directions."

Abigail fumed with resentment. "What if I don't want to go with the group?"

"If you want private lessons, we can arrange that." He patted the mare's rump and smiled at Abigail. "I'm surprised though."

"Surprised?" She met his seductive gaze and instantly regretted being so brave, afraid he could see the sharp interest she had in being tutored by him. He was fascinating even if she hated him. "By what?"

"You're tricky way of having me all to yourself."

With the ease of Clint Eastwood, he swung up into the saddle and rode off to join the troop of giggling women waiting for him.

What a phony. Nothing but gall for her, and like a true gentleman, he tipped his hat to them.

And, here she was, incapable of looking away from the blue-black of his neatly cropped hair grazing the collar of his faded plaid shirt.

Being combative with this man was pointless. She'd try to be quiet and not draw attention to herself.

There was only one problem with that way of thinking. Something about this male in worn Levi's and scuffed boots rode her nerves and roused her desire to do him bodily harm. His tongue was sharp and vulgar.

A seed of an idea spun through her mind accompanied by a pleasant tingle. There was one sure way to smash his giant ego. Seduction with no intention of fulfilling his dream was exactly what he deserved.

Might as well get started on that little chore right now.

Her head snapped back under the abrupt jolt when her mount suddenly decided to take off with no coaxing. The mare she straddled must have been hot for the dirty-mouthed trail boss, judging by the way she trotted after him. That was a good thing, because Abigail wasn't proficient with the reins yet.

He turned in the saddle to look at her, and shook his head as the damned mare rumbled to a stop beside him. Maude as he called her, blew out a long snort and sawed her head up and down as if she'd run a mile. Turk leaned on the saddle horn, eyeing Abigail with a sardonic smile.

"Now, don't things work better when you cooperate with the group?"

"Group?" Abigail arched her brows and leaned toward him. "I should have figured you were into groups?" Common sense deserted her and she gazed defiantly into his narrowed eyes. The seduction plan was nixed. He wasn't dumb enough to fall for cheap tricks. Yet.

Her plan to seduce him was dumb at best. She was out in the tumbleweed country, trying to escape the oppressive control of her grandfather. Now, here she was in the process of working her way into another bad situation with no way out other than losing her dignity.

Abigail hated to admit it, but Turk would easily chew her up and swallow without blinking. She would leave him alone and be ready when Shane Chaloun came for her.

Another wrinkle in her life. Shane. At times he was a scary individual, always into cults and science group's, hell-bent on getting to Mars. But, he had real connections with shadow people of the gambling casinos in the Midwest and cellar party's in New York and Chicago that catered to the opium pipe.

Russia was his port of call when he needed to leave the country. He ran through cash as if he had lots of it, just like she had. He didn't mind spreading cash around when he had it. Abigail wasn't sure where that money came from or what he did to get it.

Until now, she hadn't given it any thought. After thinking over everything he'd told her, she was worried about him. Maybe a little bit about herself.

All she wanted was enough to get out of the States and to buy a new identity. Shane promised her that for her knowledge of social moirés and an introduction to her friends in Europe. They were users of each other. He'd make it easier to travel without notice.

A young woman alone was a target for all kinds of evil things, mostly from men, and she'd met the first of them, Turk Gunnison. Most women would find him highly attractive and hard to refuse anything. Her only desire now was escape to another life, not be entangled in a losing affair.

As soon as she could access her personal funds, she'd repay Shane. Being in a man's debt meant nothing but pain for women.

She hadn't learned much from her mother, only that men were to be used and tricked or you paid with your very existence. So much for motherly advice and comfort. Her mother had skipped out when she was twelve, leaving Abigail with her wealthy and oppressively strict grandfather. If not for her beautiful Spanish grandmother's occasional visits, her life would have been completely dismal.

Abigail lagged behind the rest of the group, wanting to throw her boot at Turk's head. He made a point of turning in the saddle to pin her with his exotic gaze. Her feelings for him raged between icy indifference to molten desire.

She couldn't make a personal call from this damn trail ride because of ranch policy that prohibited phones. Or so he'd said the moment she'd pulled out her phone. According to Turk, the ring tones would startle and kill his animals from stress. He'd pointed to the list of rules prominently posted on just about every wall. Use the phone in the commons room of the lodge or wait until you were off the property.

A secretive smile played over her lips. Tonight, she'd teach the slave master who was in charge. He'd already made it too easy for her, not smart enough to confiscate both her phones.

He chose that moment to look back again, and motion for her to come to the front.

She feigned ignorance and stared off to her right, worry gripping her heart for a moment. The dirt road disappeared around a stand of pine trees and mammoth rocks. She wondered what lay beyond the bend in the lonely looking road.

Not put off by her pointed snub, he turning his mount around to ride back toward her. Typical male, he couldn't accept rebuff by a woman and rushed headlong in her direction to ply her with more of his studly-stuff. Leaning over to comb her fingers through the fringe of her chaps, she feigned ignorance of his approach.

He blazed his way to the back of the group, arriving by her side in a cloud of fine dust.

"Huffy." He looked extra tall and leaner than she recalled five minutes ago. "I want you to ride up front."

Suspicion shot through her. "Why?"

"You'll appreciate the scenery more if you see it without dust in your face." His smile was devious and so sensual her breasts throbbed with an ache from imagining the tug of his lips on her nipples.

"I want a drink." Her tongue was thick and dry. Sexual awareness wove through her thighs and coiled neatly in her crotch. "Now."

He smiled through the dust cloaking them and leaned over to get his canteen. "I wouldn't deprive you of anything you really need." Uncapping the flask, he tipped it to her lips.

Nothing had ever tasted sweeter, or more satisfying. Sucking on the neck where his mouth had been was enough to stir her into orgasmic fever. Why did it feel as if he'd touched her with a hot poker? She'd rather die than have sex with a loser like him. Then why was she so wet?

Her mouth opened in a wide gape of irritation when he took the canteen and immediately drank, long and deep. He grinned at her over the silver flask.

"Choke on it." She slapped the reins on the mare's neck and rode off to settle in beside Bertha.

Turk caught up, reaching out to catch her mounts bridle. "I'll show you the stream where we'll be fishing tomorrow."

"Fishing?" Abigail wanted to scream. "That sounds so lovely." Had her sarcasm been strong enough?

"I was hoping you'd like it." He patted her knee. "I'm here to please."

"So you've said a dozen times. When does it start?"

His suntanned hand rested easy on his hard thigh, and she knew her gaze could equal that of a starving hawk. Forcing her head to swivel in another direction, she saw the glisten of water in the distance.

The horses snorted and picked up their pace. She didn't blame them. This country had gotten hot and dry in late September. An added bonus came unexpectedly when Turk rode off to lead the way down the incline, waiting on the sandy shoreline while the ladies picked their way down to join him.

The mare she was on didn't need coaxing. She galloped down the trail, going straight for the water.

"Stop!" Abigail wrapped her hands around the saddle horn while the mare sucked up water.

"Huffy."

It was him again.

"Let me help you off."

He reached for her, his forearms corded with strength as his hands fit around her waist. No time to refuse. She was off the mare and sliding down the length of his body before she could breath.

"I'll ask if I ever need you for anything."

He had a multitude of things to learn about her. Too bad there wouldn't be time to break him to the bit.

Chapter 2

Turk sipped coffee from his favorite blue granite cup and paced the floor of his office. "Just what is it about this situation you find so damn funny?"

Talking to Gun, his older brother was always interesting if not amusing. Not today.

"You're my brother so I won't tell you to go to hell. You still want to know why I made my ranch into a woman's only lodge?"

On the other end of the line, Gun was laughing. "I've heard all that before. Now, tell me the truth."

Setting the cup on his gnarly old oak desk, he noticed the scars from generations of Gunnison men's spurs. They were a reminder of where he and Gun came from.

Turk tried to refuse his brother's request. "I want peace and quiet, not a horde of drunks looking for a fight. Women don't have too many choices to get away from those same assholes. So, I have what they need."

"Yeah. I know all about how you tease and please the ladies." The laughter coming from the other end of the line didn't bother Turk. His brother wasn't as hardboiled as he wanted the world to believe. "On the other hand, it's not like you to go for the chick's carrying torches for some other man."

He could see Gun needed to be educated on the finer art of being with women he didn't want to sleep with. "We're not too different, Gun. The ladies and me."

"What do you mean?" Mister Flamboyance sounded concerned. "Talk to me, Turk."

"I meant, we all need space and these women seem to be a good fit for the lodge."

"I can see that happening."

Knowing Gun was grinning ear to ear, Turk tried to answer his questions about the ranch. "I didn't give the lodge a fancy name. The women never have to worry about being found if that's what they want."

Silence for a few seconds. "So, you work them hard all day, and lights out at sundown?" He chuckled at his own humor.

"Nope. They can follow me around, fish or ride horses or whatever hits their fancy. I only have one fast rule here and they abide by it. With one exception."

"How do you ever get them to leave?" A soft cough ended the lapse in conversation. "Look, Turk. I want you to keep an eye out for the girl I told you about. Her grandfather's a client of Gunnison Security and I'd take care of this personally, but Ali's in labor right now and I can't leave town."

"I left the service to get away from conflict and I'm not liking the way you're roping me into this mess you have going." Turk chewed a few jellybeans, calming his tone. "Tell Ali I'll get back there to see her and the kids the minute I can break away." Turk laughed. "You guys ever heard of condoms?"

"Ali doesn't like them. I'm going back to the hospital in a few minutes. I have a new mouth to feed making its debut any time now." Pride resonated loud and clear in Gun's voice, them altered to out and out begging. "Come on, man. That young girl's going to get in trouble left on her own. Just let me know when she arrives, and hold her until her grandfather can make arrangements for her to go home."

"You keep saying 'she'. What's this chick's name? How am I supposed to cut her out of the herd? And what if he's a bastard and she doesn't want to go back?"

"Abigail Madonna Van Huffington." Sounded like Gun was opening a bag of chips from the crackling. "He's not a bastard, or so I hear. He's afraid she'll do something serious and end up in prison or worse. Hell, I stay out of family squabbles. If she wasn't involved with a subversive, I wouldn't touch this."

Tantrum screaming from one of his nieces pierced Turk's eardrum. Today, Gun ran herd on his brood and wasn't doing it very well. No surprise when his brother hung up with hardly a fare thee well. "Gun! Wait a damn minute."

Now what? Until five days ago, his life had settled into a calm, dependable routine that no one dared break.

Abigail. A damned sexy, spoiled malcontent. According to Gun's sketchy description, she was barely twenty-one and single, hooked up with a goofball from Canada that had managed to get on the FBI'S black list. Ass deep in trouble.

The day she'd arrived in Lone Horse was memorable to say the least, a real precursor of what was to come. She'd been perched like a movie star on her luggage, waiting for a peon to tote her gear. Dressed in a suit of white silk and funky wide-brimmed hat, shoes with no more than a string to hold them on her bare feet, Miss Huffy eyed him like he was her misbehaving pet Saluki!

Her eyes widened to saucer size when he told her to grab a couple of suitcases and follow him to the truck. Their relationship had sputtered from the beginning and finally fizzled out without taking its first giddy breath.

He walked out of his office and looked in the great room. The place was vacant except for Lucy, the British shorthair soaking up sun in the open patio doors. Damn cat had forced his hand and he'd let her stay, but only because she was big as a barrel with kittens. That should have been a warning of things to come.

Especially after Elaine, his long time girlfriend had decided she didn't want to give up the military life and gave him the big kiss goodbye. She still called him from time to time, always asking if he was ready for a conjugal visit. That meant sex. Nothing binding, just pure wild sex, which of course he was game for.

Turk gave up his commission in the Army, prepared to begin a new, sane life. His entire family had gone into shock over his decision to turn his place into a women's only, guest ranch.

He'd had a gut full of worrying about pea brain guys that were determined to get them selves killed no matter how hard he trained them.

Women, he knew, their likes and dislikes, and how to make them purr. Entertaining and watching over a bunch of ladies came natural as breathing. Women were definitely what he understood. They didn't deliberately try to provoke him and had a healthy respect for his opinion.

And, then there was Abigail.

Why the hell had she chosen his place over the dozen spas in nearby Aspen? This sure wasn't the place to get the pampering she must be accustomed to. And from what Gun had said, she had a knack for choosing scum when it came to men.

Now, she was here, in his space, waiting for her boyfriend. A troublemaker with big ideas. The last thing Turk wanted in his life or on his property was trouble, but it seemed to be hunting him down. Until he got more information on this guy Huffy had hooked up with, he'd have to keep her under close surveillance.

It struck him that if he watched her any closer, she'd be sleeping in his room. The thought wasn't at all unpleasant.

Man, her grandfather couldn't yank her out of there fast enough to suit him.

Turk stepped out onto the patio. He took a quick head count of his lady guests. Eleven pretty maids in a row. So, where was the twelfth? All accounted for except Ms. Huffy, the pain in his ass.

Turk wasn't too concerned about her taking care of herself, except she might be meeting with that punk kid while he sipped coffee.

"That'll be the day," he grumbled. Jamming his hat on his head, he stomped off the patio and across the hard packed dirt of the front yard.

The usual chattering groups of females sat in the shade, gossiping and playing cards or doing each other's nails.

He paused to watch a trio doing yoga exercises. *Damn.* There was something going on in every corner, so why couldn't Huffy find a hole to fit in?

Where was she, and what would he say when he found her? He stood gazing around for several minutes. Listening to the late summer sounds. A rich mix of bugs, birds and female's laughter. Not a bad sound at all. It was downright hypnotizing. The sweet, softness brought images of Huffy to mind.

He broke a sweat and grimaced. Controlling his libido had been ingrained in his psyche for a longtime. He learned in the military you don't fuck until the war is won. The need for sex had come from out of the blue. Yeah, sure he knew men thought of sex every other minute, but this was deep, hot and urgent.

Ticked off at his inability to cope with one little problem, Turk headed for the stable to see if she might lower herself to go there. That was the place where no one ever gave him reason to lose his temper.

Cool and fragrant, with dappled light coming from the overhead windows, the stables were always clean and reasonably quiet. Right now, Conner and Luke, the two guys that helped out around the ranch were in town picking up supplies. The place seemed deserted.

Now what? He exhaled, prepared to search the ranch top to bottom. Where to start was a problem. She wasn't the type to venture off in the woods. He heard it then, the soft murmur of a familiar, feminine voice.

He moved slowly to the door, unsure if he'd heard correctly. No, he hadn't been mistaken. Huffy was in the tack room, talking to that punk on a cell phone she'd been foxy enough to hide from him.

He got up and walked slowly to the door, listening while a hard grimace set his jaw. She rattled off instructions and directions to whoever was on the phone with her before Turk kicked the open the door.

Her scream was oddly enjoyable. A small payback for making his life a living hell.

"Get out of here!"

He threw his hat on the floor and stalked toward her. "You're giving me orders?" Glaring at the phone she clutched, he moved closer to her. "I have asked you to use the pay phone. There are good reasons for that. You're the only one who can't follow orders. Are you dumb?"

Pure indignation blazed in her glorious blue eyes. Anger colored her cheeks a bright, rosy hue. Now he realized where his urge for sex came from. He'd never wanted any woman as much as this spitting cat.

"Me? Dumb?" He almost missed her nasty rebuttal, his hungry gaze trying hard to get under the material of her gauzy, harem style pants. "You've been out here in the woods too long, Turk. There are laws against holding people as hostages."

He'd devoted a lot of time trying to forget the very people she'd just described. The sounds and scenes were slow to fade.

"Huffy. Get out of here before I tell you what a real sweetheart you are." Her pretty, soft mouth opened in surprise. "Don't say anything. Just get out. Leave that damn phone."

"I will not."

The snotty indignation in her refusal lit his torch.

He hadn't lost the Cobra quickness that had saved his life repeatedly in battle. He gripped her arm and pulled her snug against his body, reaching around to yank the phone from her waistband.

"Yes, you will." He was hard as bricks again, being sucked in by the way she seemed to melt into him, the sweet scent of her brunette hair. He almost shuddered with the force of sizzling desire.

"You're a bully." She trembled in his grip, not enough to make him look away from the globes of her ass under the lilac material. "Why don't you just come out and ask for sex?"

"Take my advice and get back to the lodge."

"Or you'll do what?"

His thoughts rampaged with a dozen explicit scenes, all starring him and Huffy in a tangle of arms and legs.

Shit! He had no answer for that, but he could get her out of the stable. "Move out. The men are bringing the horses in and you might get roughed up."

"Another threat?" She swished by him, her tight little ass working under that thin material, enticing him with its perfect shape. He could feel it in his hands. "I expect the return of my phone and that you stay away from me."

"Sorry, Huffy." He couldn't keep the grin from his mouth. She was tempting as the apple in Eden, but irritating as sand in an eye. "I still give the orders around here."

"Oh, what an honor." She made a grab for her cell phone, scowling at her empty hand. "Being CEO of a farm isn't much to be swell headed over."

Turk looked into the lush blue of her eyes, and saw little imps dancing around in their depths. "Huffy, let's go." He took a few steps, hoping she'd follow him. It was dangerous for them to be alone, anywhere, much less the stable. She was on his heels, puffing with outrage.

"If I wasn't paid up here for the next two weeks, I'd leave immediately."

"I'd be happy to give you a ride into town."

She clamped her lips together and sashayed past him, leaving him to wonder if she was as passionate in bed as she was about running roughshod over his sorry ass.

Chapter 3

Still fuming over the loss of her only private contact with the outside world, Abigail nibbled on her food, or what he called 'supper'.

Biscuits and coleslaw with fried chicken and gooseberry cobbler served in surprisingly pretty dishes. The chicken was fried golden brown and the gravy on a biscuit was heavenly with lots of pepper.

Trying to pretend she didn't like the cobbler was crazy. The brown sugared crust and tart filling was so good she closed her eyes to savor the taste.

She ate hearty, but only because she had to stay fit for travel. Plus, the food smelled so good, her stomach growled like a wild animal.

Looking through the open door of the kitchen, she watched Turk enjoying his meal at the table with the hired help. He was laughing and eating, nothing like he was with her. The sudden rush of jealousy made her swallow the wrong way and choke.

He looked out to see what was going on and because it was her, he ignored the problem. Damn him! She would never let him think she needed him for anything.

With her coughing under control, she picked up her plate and carried it into the kitchen, placing the scraps in the container beneath the huge sink. While she was there, she covertly scanned the place, hoping to see her cell phone.

Sensing a hard stare, she turned to find Turk's entrancing gaze pasted on her ass. A wave of hot embarrassment swept over her while his unwavering gaze locked on her. She fought the urge to run. There was no way to search for the phone as long as he was around.

Getting past the table was hard, especially with him staring at her. She realized now, his stare was not lustful, only pure calculating suspicion. He didn't like her. Sure, she was pretty certain he wanted to take her clothes off, but he disliked her intensely.

He kicked the door shut as soon as she left the kitchen, his actions speaking loud and clear without saying a word.

She had to get out of this place before doing something to or with Turk that would ruin her chances of ever seeing real freedom.

Hot resentment, along with a chill of worry, coursed through her body. Why was she on the run with no hope and no cash? This had to be the perfect plot for a tearjerker, afternoon movie. Not that she'd been allowed to see many of them.

She took a quick account of her life. Twenty-one, graduate of Wellesley, degree in fine arts and language, not to mention European history, hiding out in the sagebrush until her schizoid friend brought money. Her mother would be proud of her.

The pay phone hung on the wall near the entry door. A table had been placed there, and stocked with colorful pens and plenty of note pads. Placed around the table were several chairs to sit in while making your call. The clincher was the varnished, Chinese privacy screens and plants around to make a caller feel at ease.

Walking to the phone, she dug in her wallet for change. It seemed that would be unnecessary. There was a small fortune in change in a bowl for the guest' convenience.

Now she didn't have a leg to stand on if she decided to bring charges against him.

She glanced toward the open kitchen door. Would using the pay phone make her the loser in their ongoing differences? That didn't matter now. She dropped the required coins in the slot, and quickly dialed Shane's number.

While waiting for him to answer the phone, Abigail tapped her foot. At last, he answered her call.

"Shane. What have you been doing? What's been happening?"

He stuttered, sounded nervous, not anything new, but far more noticeable today. "I'll be a few days longer getting out there."

She wanted to scream. "You mean I'm stuck here in Goon Gorge and you can't tell me exactly how much longer?"

"Sorry, Abbey. But, your family put a tail on me."

"That's ridiculous. My grandfather doesn't care enough to do that. Can't you lose whoever it is?"

"It's not that simple." She heard him swallow and it sounded painful. "I got into some trouble at work. I left without going to the meeting I was supposed to attend. They're trying to find me."

She forgot to modulate her voice. "I can't believe how much trouble you're always in. I need your help to get across the border to Puerto Vallarta." She hugged the phone box, pressing her forehead against the wall. "Shane, please try to understand. I'll never make it out of the country unescorted."

"I'm sorry, Abbey."

"I'm sorry too." Abigail struggled to withstand the crush of worry threatening to end her bid for freedom. "If I can get to Puerto Vallarta, my Grandmother will help me get to London."

Shane exhaled hard, his voice shaking. "I hate to disappoint you, Abbey, but I have to take care of something before I come for you."

"Don't you dare make me wait any longer than absolutely necessary." Her voce shook with emotion.

"I'll be there. Just not when we planned."

"You're letting me down!" She clenched her teeth against a hiss of desperation. "Why? What's happened?"

"I can't tell you now. I'll come for you, so just sit tight."

Her hushed words were poignant pleas for help. "No. No, I can't do this any longer, Shane. Don't you understand I have a job waiting in London? The travel agency won't hold that position open until I just happen to feel like showing up for work!"

He didn't hear her protest. He'd hung up, leaving her holding a silent receiver. It was childish, but Abigail slammed the phone into the hook, several times.

"He must've hung up."

The voice drawled over her stretched nerves like hot syrup.

"You eavesdrop as well?" Her lips barely moved over her clenched teeth.

"Don't have to when you bellow like a little bull."

There were thousands of things she wanted to say. She chose the least incendiary. "I won't mention what part of the bull anatomy you most resemble."

He walked away, stopping at the door of his private quarters. "I'll try to figure it out." His gaze played over the bare skin of her midriff. "Better wear something that covers your hide tomorrow."

"Don't worry about my hide." She tossed the card in the change bowl. "You'll never have to brand the thing."

Any other time or place, his smile would have had her seduced, undressed and loving it. Not today. Yet, she couldn't fight the seductive stroke of his voice.

"You're such a tease, Huffy." His gaze hardened. "I'm serious. See to it you wear sturdier clothing tomorrow."

"I'm not doing any chores as you call them. I don't know how to milk cows, and I don't plow."

His expression said plenty, mostly how amusing he found her. "Stop pretending you don't like me. I'll teach you some new things tomorrow."

Her imagination went wild. "I will not be alone with you if that is your plan." Her heart pounded with anticipation.

"Hell, Huffy." He laughed out loud. "I was talking about fishing. You have a dirty mind, woman."

He left her to her thoughts and went into his quarters. Better to leave it alone, she thought. He always won the verbal skirmishes.

There was no way out of the current mess she was in. except wait. And, Turk would make every minute sheer hell if she let him. She went up to her room, wondering how much he'd heard.

It didn't matter. He was just an ignorant cowboy she could handle or ignore if she chose to.

Her room in the lodge was small and Spartan to her way of thinking. The full sized bed took up most of the space, leaving room only for a small dressing table and tiny nightstand. The closet barely held the clothes she'd brought. Every drawer in the tiny French stack chest was filled to capacity.

The window overlooking the front yard was the single luxury. She could see Turk coming and going. It had become an addiction to know where he was at all times.

"Fool." She flopped onto the bed and breathed deep. The place smelled of fresh air and Turk. He permeated everything, everywhere, all the time. The sheets and towels, and her tongue.

"Idiot." She threw her sandal at the closet door, consumed with self-disgust. There had been men in her life, none hot as Turk, but several came close.

What was wrong with her? He was nothing but trouble and if she didn't watch herself, he'd make her forget why she'd come to his barren lodge. She had to stop comparing the stag to the men she knew. Yet, she couldn't help wondering about his body and how strong he would be while making love. Being without a lover for most of the year had finally borne the fruit of being horny.

Of course, she would be a stranger wherever she went now. It took time to find a suitable partner and she wasn't sure her hormones would stabilize enough to allow selection. "Stop it! You're thinking like a science fiction bitch!"

From the common room, the irresistible sound of laughter drifted up to rouse her interest. She'd not planned on going down to Sasha Brown's belly dance class, but she was too restless to stay in her room.

The music was compelling. What harm was there in enjoying herself for a few minutes? Quickly changing into a pink lounge pant and white t-shirt, Abigail sought out companionship, appropriately barefoot in deference to the no shoes dress code.

The *ching-ching* sound of the coin belt draping her hips led her down the path to become part of the sensual music.

She arrived in time to see several of the women trying to master the seductive movements. Abigail stepped into line and took up the steps, thrusting and swiveling her hips in a dance as old as Adam and Eve. After several minutes, she spotted a photo of Turk and several other men on a table next to the huge stone fireplace. They were all in military uniform, everyone, to the last man, big and filled with the devil if she knew men at all.

That was probably why he was so evil, all that gore and guns. She shivered with embarrassing excitement. The throbbing music worked like an aphrodisiac.

Unable to resist, Abigail stepped out of line to more closely examine the pictures placed on the polished buffet. Her eyes were irresistibly drawn to Turk. A throbbing sensation forced her to cross her legs. Like it or not, the maddening pulse increased whenever Turk was around.

Taking in the room, she calculated it had been so long since sex, she could legally call herself virgin. And the orgasmic music was doing nothing to make her forget that dreary statistic.

Slipping away wasn't difficult. The group had gathered around a bowl of popcorn and a big box of chocolates. Another of Turk's methods of keeping his herd submissive.

At the top of the stairs, she could see her door and the light from her nightstand lamp. Someone was in her room. Throwing caution aside, she hit the door, a glare pasted on her face. Stunned for a split second, she recovered and spoke icily to the intruder.

"What are you doing? Didn't my check clear the bank?"

Turk obviously didn't feel guilty about being caught in her room. "I brought your phone back. Minus all batteries."

"I don't think that's the real reason." She stepped into the trap and he snapped it shut.

"You toss out wide rope of invitation, Huffy." He was close enough for her to count the threads in the material of his shirt. "If you want me to stay, I will."

Damn him. The loathsome fact dawned on her. To her shame, he sensed the way her body reached for him. She must look like a cheap thrill.

"You have the wrong woman in mind, Turk." She took the stripped phone and threw it on the floor. "Don't you cowboys ride off for town when your pants get too tight?"

She hated him for laughing, hated herself for wanting to shut the door and have him all to herself all night long.

"Huffy, you've been reading too many novels. They only do that in Green Frog, Arkansas and Red Mange, Montana."

Backing up to press against the door, she eyed him with a mixture of emotions, hot desire and cold anger. "Go somewhere else to take care of that problem." He strolled by her, his grin driving her crazy. "I should report you for being a menace to your female guests."

He turned and tossed one of her sandals at her. "You're the only one complaining." Jerking his thumb to the lower level, he had the last word. "You can call anybody you want to on that phone provided for guests."

His gaze toyed with her nipples, and she thrust out her chest for his hot inspection. Sure, she wasn't going to sleep that night, but neither would he.

Chapter 4

He almost tore the door off the shower stall the next morning. Getting relief from the load of pressure weighing down his balls consumed him.

Turk never resorted to jerking off if there was another choice. This morning, he took control of the aching monster with his right hand.

Tense from days of wanting to crawl all over Huffy, nights of erotic dreams humbled him to self-service. Working his cock felt damned good.

Tonight would probably call for more palm therapy after spending another day with her. From now on, those chicks could find their own entertainment.

Bracing one hand on the wall, he pressed his forehead against it, exhaling hard as the image of her sweet ass bounced through his mind. His libido brought him more delicious tidbits, the full, soft warmth of her breasts and flat belly. His fingers flexed as he imagined her curvaceous hips gyrating against his dick.

Aw, damn it was getting good. The heaviness in his bag and hot jolts of approaching come gripped his body. Flexing his thighs until the muscles of his ass bunched in rock solid mass, he threw back his head while the pressure erupted in the spray of the shower. The release robbed his legs of strength, forcing him to lean against the wall.

Thanks to the powerful, rushing hiss of the spray, his groan didn't escape the bathroom to frighten the women or the wildlife. It seemed this was his last outpost of privacy, or escape from temptation Huffy shoved in his face.

That thought pissed him off. He was not some teen, bed-wetting kid she could jerk around by his dick.

Abigail Van Huffington was phenomenal to look at, to stare at and probably to fuck. She smelled like Persian Lilac, light and sweet in the warmth of day. Heady, like honeyed wine at night. Her skin was smooth and the color of the sand he'd seen somewhere in the Caribbean. Warm and unblemished.

He wondered about her breasts. Sure it was stupid, and he would regret it later. Fantasizing about her would bring him nothing but rock-aches.

He grabbed a clean shirt and jeans, yanking shorts and socks from his chest of drawers. Boots on, freshly shaved, and hair combed, he wondered how long it would take Huffy to reduce him to a sweaty, weak-legged fool.

Before going to the kitchen for breakfast, Turk stopped off at his small office to check the messages on the fax.

Gun's fax was three pages long. Almost certain the news was bad, he took the note to his desk and sat down to read.

His scowl deepened as he read the report on what he dubbed the odd couple. Only one of the pair really interested him. His gaze flicked over the type until Abigail's name jumped out at him

He tried to concentrate on the importance of the words, not scour the page for information on her. He'd come back to her.

Right now, the punk named Shane was under the microscope. Twenty-five, Canadian schools, until he arrived in Dallas a year ago. Always in the middle of any demonstration against authority. *Just great.*

He scooped up a handful of jellybeans and popped them in his mouth. It didn't stop the pounding of his heart when he read she hadn't been exactly a wallflower. She'd been the main squeeze of a Dallas detective, a NHL hockey player, and a professional bull rider. He grimaced. She liked them on the tough side.

He propped his feet on the desk, chewing the sugar charged candy. Puzzled by the relationship between Shane and Huffy, he checked vital statistics again. He smirked a little when he read Shane was barely five-foot seven. Was never involved in sports, and destitute by her standards. He came from modest means. His parents had emigrated from Russia to Canada. Both mother and father taught biology at a College in Toronto. This sucker had to be a junior Einstein and his penchant for getting into trouble excited her.

Thudding sounds on the stairway meant the ladies were up and ready for the day. Turk wasn't sure he wanted to tackle what it had in store.

He put the letter aside and went out to see what they had in mind. There was plenty of time to find out Miss Abigail's full history. Probably lots more than he wanted to know.

He wanted to laugh at the array of crap the women were dragging downstairs. Hats, blankets and umbrellas along with the ever-present handbags. Instead, he smiled and gestured to their picnic baskets.

"Good morning. Ready to go, I see."

They all giggled and pushed Bertha to the front. She wasn't shy.

"Yes we are, but Abigail is lagging behind." Bertha made a pouting face. "Must we wait on her? My father said, always fish before the sun was high."

Who would have thought of that but Bertha? "Nothing says Abigail is required to go along."

Every face that stared at him beamed with happiness as the women shook their heads in agreement to his comment. Did they dislike her that much? Maybe they had taken a cue from his big mouth.

"Ladies. Have your breakfast. I'm sure she'll come down and be ready to go soon."

A collective 'aw shit' sound rose from the group. Bertha waved a hand in dismissal of the idea. "She's coming down now." Grabbing her straw hat, she left with the group heading for the dining room.

Turk took a step to follow them, stopped when a glimmer of what heaven would be like, blinded him to reality. Huffy was halfway down the stairs, dressed in cherry red chaps over white jeans and a scanty red halter.

She was damned fabulous and looking at him with veiled contempt.

* * * *

The last thing Abigail wanted was more sweat and the smell of fishy water in the hot sun. She was deeply disappointed in Shane, and longed to find a place to scream out her misery.

Right now, the owner of the prison facility eyed her with impatience and a hint of desire. He wanted in her pants. No surprise there, but something else lurked under that tanned hide.

How many women had he ruined for life because of his way with a strong hand and soft drawl? She'd had tough men as lovers. None of them possessed Turk's calm gaze or the roaring undercurrent of male power his presence shouted.

How hard was it going to be, cutting this Sampson's hair?

Looking away from Turk required some effort. His gaze grabbed her hard. Her imagination went in a spin, feeling pressure from his fingers that must be leaving prints on her breast.

A loose plan formed in her resentful heart. *Make Turk want you so much his tongue falls out. Starting now.*

"Good morning." Careful to be a little aloof, she kept a cool head. Anything more would make this big wolf suspicious. "Am I in time for the trip?"

His level gaze shifted from her face to the bare skin of her midriff. "Just in time." He smiled and stood his ground, forcing her to slide by him.

The very scent of him touched her like tongues of warm silk.

"I'll just run in and see if the others want me to help." With deliberate seduction, she pulled her hair over her shoulder to stroke it as if it were a cat.

"Huffy." He had a ravenous look in his eyes. "They don't need help. The guys are getting things ready outside."

"Really?" She arched her brows, aware he was keeping her away from the group. She wanted to know why. "Maybe the cook could use a hand?"

"Stay here a minute." He turned and went into his office, seeming to be quite sure she would be waiting when he came back. Okay, this gave her a chance to stare at his great looking rear. She felt no shame while completely devouring him as he walked away.

How could a man look so good in worn jeans and weather beaten cornflower blue shirt? His hair was so black she could only think of a Texas storm at night. Nothing but a little hands-on time could describe his strong, broad shoulders and the lean waist above a pair of hard buns. Her mind painted images of him, nude, aroused and smiling.

Shrugging away the warm, mental sex measurements, Abigail left the entry hall, and headed for the kitchen.

She looked over her shoulder to find Turk gazing at her. He seemed to have difficulty speaking his mind, holding a flower festooned straw hat out to her.

"What's this?"

"You wont like getting sunburned." His gaze dipped to her breasts and lingered. "Might require a medic."

Now was not the time to tell him she had a cute little hat from Bergdorff's department store in New York.

"Well, I don't know what to say. Thank you." Her lashes lowered in a show of proper modesty as she glanced down shyly.

"No thanks needed. It gets hot on the water." His half smile was more cynical than kind.

Damn it! He wasn't buying her sweet display. Not yet. Tricking him into becoming fond of her might require sex. At least the promise of it.

Damndest thing. Her blood sizzled while her thighs pulsed crazily. There was nothing she could do about the high blush on her cheeks. She always flushed rosy when sexually excited and Turk could have taken her right there against the wall.

"Huffy." His expression showed concern for a split second. "You ailing?"

"No." She flung her hair away from her neck.

He moved and she was done in by the scent of oriental spice and violets. Her female voice shrieked at her. *Lick him! Bury your nose in his neck!*

"You'd better stay close to me today."

He may as well have told her to strip.

"I could stay here."

His eyes narrowed. "I'll bring you back if need be."

Well, there went her chance to call Shane. He was forcing her hand, and seducing him might be a real problem. He saw her as a nuisance and that wasn't exactly conducive to hot sex.

What happened after the seduction would be even harder to pull off.

Abigail looked up to meet his steady gaze. "You're probably right. The Van Huffington women have always had a terrible time with heat and vapors."

She wanted to laugh out loud when he shook his head and playfully tugged her ponytail.

"I somehow find that hard to believe."

He didn't seem to want to talk any more after that, and walked outside.

"I didn't mean to scare you." She ran behind him, waving the silly straw hat to get his attention.

"I'll get your mount ready today. After this, you saddle your own." Turk brought out the horse she'd been assigned, and eyed her over the mares back. "Why don't you ride any better? You're from Arizona, aren't you?"

It took great restraint not to roll her eyes and lecture him. "I wasn't allowed to act like a boy."

He grinned at her, and for the first time, he could have been flirting with her. "And I'm damn glad of that."

She could barely stand, horse flies sounded like tinkling bells and the smell of sweat was a new kind of elixir.

He led the stoic mare to where Abigail stood on straw legs. When he handed her the reins, their fingers brushed intimately, striking a firestorm of red-hot liquid pheromone in her body. Glancing up, her gaze rested on the open collar of his shirt, and her heart went crazy. His neck looked strong where his skin had been exposed to the sun, and how many pairs of lips? She didn't care right then. Abigail forced her gaze to the reins he'd handed her.

"I'll try not to be trouble today." She tried to sound demure, but how the hell could she when her crotch throbbed like a machine.

"Just don't go off by yourself. Bears, you know."

Chapter 5

It was a damn good thing the stable doors had been open, or Huffy would be wearing him and nothing else right now. Turk spent a lot longer than usual getting the tack room straightened up. Miss Huffy had left him with lead in his shorts.

"Turk!"

Aw, why did they always yell like that? He grabbed his hat and swatted the front of his pants. Hell, they'd all seen boners before.

Outside, he looked around, cussing under his breath after noticing his horse that had been tied to the hitching post, now ran down the road hell-bent for freedom.

The expression on Huffy's face screamed guilt. "All right. Who cut that horse loose?"

She hesitantly lifted her hand. "I was going to bring him to you."

"You can go after him now." He scowled, pissed off at himself for wanting to hug her and tell her it was okay. "Well?"

"I can't catch him." She lifted her shoulders in a show of resignation.

Looking from her to the cursed horse getting smaller in the distance, Turk gestured toward her. "Get on that mare."

She stumbled and fell against the horse before he could help her.

Huffy was delicate in his hands, but he had no time to enjoy it. He lifted her onto the saddle and swung up behind her. Tapping the horse's flanks with the toe of his boot, the docile animal took off like a rocket.

Hot damn, this was fun. A blooded horse under him and a screaming chick in his arms. Huffy was a sweet weight bumping against his crotch. Her round bottom lifted off the saddle and slid down his cock every time the mare's hoofs hit the ground.

He hugged her close and gave their mount her head, inhaling the soft fragrance of the fair damsels hair that whipped across his face.

The stallion soon tired of running and slowed to a frisky trot and the mare pulled up next to him.

Brushing her ponytail out of his face, Turk growled in her ear. "I thought you said no trouble today."

She eyed him over her shoulder, her cheeks flushed and eyes sparkling. "I said I'd try."

Dismounting probably was the best choice he could make at the moment. He didn't have time to hit an icy shower again. From a few feet away, his stallion stared at him as if thinking of bolting again.

Turk approached him; sweet-talking the spirited animal from long habit, forgetting Huffy could hear him. He held his hand out, his voice soothing and coddling.

"Easy, my man. I'm here now." Catching the fancy studded bridle, he stroked the horse's nose. "Good boy. Don't go running off like that. You might get hurt."

He led the stallion to where Huffy sat, observing the proceedings, and couldn't help the tingle of nerves flashing over his body.

She gazed at him with a hint of a smile that he couldn't figure. Probably thought he was weird and a freaking idiot. Maybe he was. Yet, what she thought didn't matter. Plain fact was, no horse on this property would ever be afraid of him.

His father raised the best saddle horses in Texas and never lifted a hand in anger to his stock. He always said a quiet word worked a lot faster than a whip. Like most always, his dad had been right.

The stallion nickered and shied back a few steps.

Maybe it had been one of those perfect timing things, him turning exactly right as to catch the suns glint off something metallic in the hills.

Weapon. Where's my weapon?

Reason cleared away the blink of panic. He was home in Lone Horse, not some hellhole sand pile.

Just the same, he'd have a look.

"Huffy." He mounted up, nodded in the direction of the lodge. "You go back to the house and wait with the other ladies."

She looked shocked, her rounded, morning glory eyes staring at him in disbelief. "I will not. I'm afraid to go down that road alone."

"Hell." He grimaced. This female was never going to be anything but trouble. "Come on, but don't give me reason to put a choke hold on you."

He couldn't believe she'd merely clamped her lips tight over her teeth instead of arguing. Almost.

"Choke hold, my rear. You just try it!"

He chuckled at her threat. "Stow it, lady. Let's go."

They rode single file off the road, following a trail heavily shadowed by sweeping pines and house sized boulders. Turk's thoughts still lingered on his sour faced companion.

If he hadn't seen that sun flare, he might still have Huffy sitting on his saddle horn.

* * * *

Abigail stopped grumbling under her breath and eased back in the saddle, emulating the relaxed way Turk sat his horse. This was a far different scene than she'd imagined for their first time alone.

Right now, he should be crushing her lips with his, forcing his hard body into hers. Ha! What a laugh.

Up ahead of her was a man with something on his mind, just not her.

A handful of pebbles rolled down the hillside from above the trail. A lurch of fear gripped her stomach when he leaned over and pulled a rifle from the scabbard on his saddle.

"Where'd that come from?" She wheezed out the question in surprise and fright. His stare was clear warning to shut her mouth. That didn't stop her. "I mean it. Put that thing away."

Backing his horse up to glare directly at her, Turk caught her arm. "I told you to go back to the lodge. You're here by your own stubborn bitchiness." His horse moved sideways and he held on, almost pulling her off the saddle. "What did I say about being trouble?"

"Take your hand off my arm." The glint of anger in his eyes didn't worry Abigail. The ice of his words did. "Tell me what's going on."

He righted her on the horse and shook his head. "If its what I think, you're in big trouble."

"Me?"

"You."

She shook her head, the tremble on her lips barely discernable. "You're making this up."

"Why the hell would I do that?"

"You don't like me and will do anything to irritate me."

He grabbed the mare's reins. "You're right. I don't much like you. On the other hand, I don't waste time trying to piss off chicks."

Her attempt to take the reins from him failed. "Okay, then tell me what's going on. You're scaring me."

He seemed to relent a little, meeting her gaze with cool indifference. "Why did you come to Lone Horse, this lodge?"

What had made him ask that out of the blue? "I needed a place to think things over."

"What things?"

"That's none of your affair."

The sardonic smile on his mouth fit perfectly into the scene. "Everything on this ranch is my affair." He squeezed her knee. "Start talking. I want to know all about that egghead boyfriend."

Abigail opened her mouth to laugh, only to see the mistake it would be. He hadn't asked all that to be flirtatious.

"I don't know who you're talking about."

"Been that many, huh?"

"You make it sound so vulgar."

"I'm not trying to pick you up at your favorite bar."

"That would have been useless on your part. Now, back to your interrogation. I still have no idea what you're talking about."

The chiseled line of his jaw set hard as he stared at her. "I know you have a dumb-ass boyfriend lurking around like a love sick hog. You'd better tell me what's supposed to come down, lady or he's going to be hurt. Real bad."

"If you're referring to Shane, who would want to hurt him?" Images of a smallish Shane being torn to shreds by Turk frightened her. "You're just trying to frighten me."

"Just trying to save that pretty hide of yours. Maybe your boyfriends too."

He was frightening her, yet she had to keep her mouth shut. After all, he probably didn't have any real information. He was simply guessing. He'd seen enough women on the run and leaving bad situations to know all the signs. He wasted his time trying to get her to talk.

"Get over yourself. I know these horses think you're tough, but I don't."

He scowled at her for a second before tossing the reins at her. "Zip it up."

She knew what he meant and this time she did exactly that.

Abigail stopped grumbling under her breath and relaxed a little. This was a far different scene than she'd imagined for their first time alone.

Right now, Turk should be crushing her lips with his, forcing her to kiss him, and pushing his hard body into hers. Ha! Up ahead was a man with something on his mind, just not her.

Her rebellion quieted and a wisp of fear drifted around her. She'd never held a firearm in her life, and was amazed and a bit frightened by the cock-sure way Turk handled the rifle.

Remembering the pictures of him and his friends in uniforms made her feel a little better. Something about this striking cowboy made her think of Superman.

Unwilling to let him out of her sight, she followed him under a stand of old pines, their branches blocking out the sun. He must have decided she was supposed to follow his lead.

"We're going on foot from here."

She couldn't move. The muscles of her legs locked and she couldn't dismount. "I can't do it." She looked at him for help.

For once he didn't criticize or insult her, merely reached up to pull her off the horse.

"Lighten up. You'll be okay."

"Thanks."

He took her hand, sending a thrill of romantic crazies through her like a whiplash. It was powerful and mind-boggling. Not to mention, totally without romantic intent.

The same could be said of his next utterance to her.

"How long you booked at the lodge?" His delivery didn't exactly invite her to extend her stay. "I just wondered if we'd get to the top this hill by the time you check out."

"Oh, shut up." She yanked her hand from his. "I didn't ask to come with you, and I won't be here next week."

"Aw, gee. Just when I thought we might have something going."

She wanted to scream but quietly ground out her rebuttal. "God as my witness, I can't wait to get away from you."

"Okay, Scarlet." He eyed her with scorn. "Hold the horses while I do a recon run."

"A what?"

"It's party time."

"For what?"

"Close your eyes and click you heels together."

The man hated her with as much heat as she held for him. A shiver of something ran through her body. The emotion was easily identifiable. Desire, raw and explosive took her over completely. Now, she hated herself for the gnawing hunger for him she couldn't rid herself of.

Don't let him know how your libido is screaming for his touch. Get on with it. "I could seriously hate you."

"Now you're talking. I'll be back before your ruby slippers start to hurt your cute little feet."

Chapter 6

Turk hesitated to leave Huffy alone, even stopped several times to listen in case she called his name. He shoved off and crested the hill quickly, using the cover of a laurel bush to scan the valley and nearby hills.

Nothing stirred except ground squirrels and a raccoon rooting around for food. He decided to move on, stopping when his toe loosened a cigarette package. He saw red. No one was allowed to smoke up here, not ever. Closer inspection convinced him this person wasn't from Lone Horse.

He hunkered down and studied the fancy paper. He knew she didn't smoke, but Huffy came to mind instantly. Yanking off his hat, he threw it on the ground.

What the hell was she up to? More to the point, her fucking boyfriend?

He stood and grimaced in frustration, shaking his head at his feral dislike of a man he'd never met. With everything that had been going on, he naturally connected her to trouble.

That's when he noticed her climbing up toward him. She looked scared. The idea of visiting Glenda at Blue Bears Balls to take the edge off flew out the window.

"Psst." She heard him and paled, finally pinpointing his position a few yards from her. "I'll come down there."

Pebbles loosed from the moist dirt as he came back down, clattering against tree trunks and large stones. He moved quickly, unafraid of the steep decent.

She held her hand out. "I heard a terrible noise and soon after that, a horse ran past me, missing me by inches. I hid until I was sure it was gone."

"You did the right thing. We get drifters up here from time to time." As if they did it every day, he put his arm around her waist and walked her back to their horses. "The ladies at the lodge are probably pretty put out with us by now."

"I don't doubt that."

He could see lingering fear in her eyes. "Come on. The sun's just right for catching fish." He grinned and helped her mount. "By the way, it's a rule here. You clean what you catch."

"Well, I won't have to worry about that, will I?"

He must be severely demented. All he wanted to do was kiss her until he couldn't stand up and she went soft and willing in his arms. He'd broken a longtime rule. You don't ever get involved with the troublemakers. Hell, he'd been involved with Huffy from their first eye contact.

He was attracted to her vinegary toughness and endless ways to draw him into conversation. She looked like fluff, but underneath all that finery was pure bedrock. The lady could stand up to him and never blink. He liked that.

They could have made it back to the lodge in half the time, but Turk was in no hurry to lose her in the crowd. Honestly, he'd forgotten the fishing trip and would have preferred showing Huffy a few more things. He scoffed at his own ignorance. She saw him as just one of the hands, shoveling horseshit for her pleasure.

Remember who she is and what she's doing here. The chick can't wait to get away from you.

His hair prickled with an inner warning. He couldn't let her leave yet, not until he talked to Gun. Hell, why had he answered the damn phone the day his presuming brother had called?

He could feel her gaze on his back, and he kicked his horse into a gallop. Hopefully, Ali'd had the baby and Gun would be home.

Glancing back at her, he liked the way she followed suit and didn't seem scared of letting the mare have a loose rein. It figured. Things were getting better just in time to go south.

She had also taken on a more independent attitude, riding to the stable and dismounting with no help from him. They'd arrived back too late to ride with the others.

Turk walked their horses into the stable and unsaddled them. She'd gone to the house, probably to primp.

While he waited on her majesty to come outside, he decided to touch base with Gun. As a last minute precaution, he checked the staircase, making sure Huffy wasn't within earshot while he made his call.

While he waited for the connection, Turk thumbed through the bookings ledger. He sat down with a heavy sigh, rubbing his aching shoulder.

This could be good or it could be very bad. The guest book was clear in seven days. No more bookings until September. That meant peace and quiet for the rest of the summer.

"Hello. What the hell you been doing, Gun?" Understanding his brother was difficult with all the background noise. "What?"

"I said I'm changing your nephew's diaper. The one that looks and acts so much like you." He must be wrestling with the little guy from the sounds of it. "What's going on? That girl still with you?"

"Hey, brother." Turk leaned back and groaned. "This place is emptying out next week, that's what's happening. That includes 'the girl'."

"What's that?" More children's laughter and screams of an obvious good time. "You have to keep her there or my ass is cooked."

"What do you mean, your ass is cooked? I won't hold her against her will. They light you up for things like that."

Gun laughed at his impassioned announcement. "Try using that Gunnison machismo. Don't tell me she can't stand the sight of you."

"That pretty much sums it up." Turk stood and went to the door, checking to see if Huffy was malingering nearby. "I think her boyfriend's hound dogging her, but he isn't the one that worries me."

"The bad guy he's been dealing has been seen in Bermuda, hooking up with a new mule for his classified documents business." A rattle of paper sounded light years away. "We're after the top weasel, Kufu Rama Fa. He always works alone on his murder missions. He's never left a witness or link to his partners, no connections. Period."

"That's your sneaky way of telling me, he wants Huffy snuffed too. Right?"

"Exactly." A heavy silence crushed the oxygen from the room. "Her friend as well. Shane."

"That's one large name for a trouble making fink like him, to be called." Vivid, smiling images of his highly decorated, war hero cousin Shane, took center stage for a second.

"Yeah, I know." Gun must have been pacing, the hollow sound of boots on wood for a time, then thuds on carpet drew a picture of what was happening in Dallas where he took care of his children.

"Okay, so tell me exactly what Shane stole. And what did he do with it?" Turk pulled the cap from a pen with his teeth, waiting for information. "Shoot."

"You're going to laugh when you hear this."

"He's dealing with a Mid-Eastern enemy agent?" *No way.* Something really dangerous was going on out there and it hovered around Huffy.

Gun laughed the way he always did when he wasn't really amused. Low and cynical. "Our Mister Shane thinks he's saving the world by carrying secrets for our friend, Kufu Rama Fa. He's not involved in the actual theft, but doesn't seem to understand just being an associate and playing delivery boy hurts his credibility."

Turk heard light footsteps on the stairs outside the door. *Huffy.*

"Gun, fax all that crap to me, and I mean, all of it. I have to know what and who I'm dealing with."

"Affirmative." Another deep silence. "Want me to send reinforcements? I can have boots on the ground there in two hours."

"I can handle this if you get me what I need." The front screen door slammed. She'd gone outside. "How many are coming?"

"Two. Mister Big and some muscle."

He scowled, remembering their earlier conversation. "Is there anything to worry about concerning her grandfather? Sounded to me like he was pretty damned determined to haul her back to Texas."

Gun groaned. "I had to threaten him with arrest to get his attention. But, he understands the danger and wants us to handle it. Her reputation would be toast if it ever got out that she was consorting with that kind of men. He wants to do this without the FBI coming in."

"We're on a Handled By Officer situation?"

"Your decision is the only one that counts."

"I really don't want to go there again."

"Buck up, Turk. It may come to nothing more than you keeping an eye on Miss Huffington."

He looked out the window to see Huffy holding the blasted cat. When was Lucy going to have those kittens? Probably while he was gone, and where he couldn't find them.

The call ended with Gun promising to call back later that night. The only good news was that Ali was going home in the morning with their new baby girl.

He grabbed his hat from the desk and followed Huffy out to the patio. She hugged Lucy, and then held the cat out to him.

"She probably should stay inside today." Her hands were gentle while she patted on the purring cats belly. "She's near delivery.""

"I thought as much." He'd noticed the felines mammaries looking more balloon like each day. "I'll put her in the laundry room where she won't get into trouble, and hope she stays there."

He carried her to the house, taking her to the area she was supposed to stay in. Flopping down in a splash of sunlight that warmed the tile floor, Lucy turned her back on him.

"See that you have those kittens before I get back."

She got to her feet and strutted out, probably looking for the cleanest chair to use as a nursery. *Damn it.*

He paused in the door, eyeing the woman that had the perfect chemistry to blow up his plans. From where he stood, she appeared nervous, fussing with the soft fringe of her chaps. She looked startled hearing the creak of the screen door.

How did trouble and idiots with weapons always find him? Here he stood, a man with ten defenseless women and a pregnant cat to protect. Just like the Army, only a lot tougher.

Okay, time to go have fun. He stepped off the patio and motioned to his dusty, black Hemi parked near the hitching post. "Let's roll, Huffy. Conner and Luke have probably eaten their lunch and ours." She gazed at him as if she didn't understand him. "The truck. Get in."

Well, something was up with her. Damned if he knew what. He shot a fast but thorough look at her, reaffirming that nothing could possibly be wrong with her gorgeous body or her soft cherry mouth. Burning with disappointment, he fired the truck up and spun the tires to ease his mounting tension.

Chapter 7

The truck sped along and Turk seemed to be preoccupied with things other than her. She'd caught his gaze in the rearview mirror several times, but he quickly darted his attention to something else.

He'd acted nonchalant up in the hills, but had hurried her out of there for some reason, and not just because he didn't like her.

Her thoughts turned instantly to Shane and her manipulating grandfather. After her grandfather's heart attack, she'd been too ashamed to argue with him, much less leave the country for a job.

In his eyes, everything she did was selfish and never good enough. Always screaming at her to do better, to be independent, only to shackle her to his ankle with horrible comments that she didn't respect or love him, that he'd die soon and she'd be free.

She stayed out of pure guilt until she'd overheard him on the phone, conducting a search for a proper husband for her. That drove her out of the house and away from his protection.

Confiding in Shane had been her only support while she ran from apartment to apartment, and finally to Lone Horse. Her mother was unavailable, too busy playing in the surf of San Tropez.

What a spaced out family. It was no mystery to her why she'd never make herself a slave to a husband. She wouldn't put a child through the hell she'd been raised in. That kind of thing rubbed off on you.

She bit her lip and fought nausea, thinking about the mess she'd made of her life. Why had she thrown in with that little weasel, Shane? From the first, she'd seen through his bravado and outright lies of success stories.

Confronted with what she felt about him, he'd laughed and told her about his life. He considered his parents dullards and left home and family as soon as college was finished.

Shane longed for, and believed he'd attain fame and notoriety. Now, it looked like he'd do just that, but he'd picked the wrong man to aggravate.

"What's on your mind?"

Turk's unexpected question startled Abigail. "Nothing. Why do you ask?"

He glanced at her, and then shrugged. "You're hiding something."

"You're being ridiculous." A quiver of cold anxiety ran over her body.

"What's with you and that boy?"

He was smug, and cold. "Now you're just being stupid."

He made a face of out and out disgust, rolling his eyes and compressing his lips. "I'm going to dig up all your little secrets, Huffy. Already know a lot of them."

He narrowed his eyes and leaned against the door, steering with one hand. "I don't know what you're jabbering about." She wanted to claw his arm and make him hurt like she did.

"Jabbering?" Naturally she'd chosen the wrong terminology and his scorching glare was a clue. "I've tried talking straight to you. I'm through being nice."

She laughed and lifted her hands in a show of being overwhelmed. "Nice! You've done nothing but try to intimidate me from the moment you met me at the airport."

"I had you figured out before supper."

"Supper. You hick!"

He averted his eyes for a while before deciding to break the icy wall between them. "I'm not going to argue with you anymore. But I'll be around."

"Oh, you're always around." Her fingers plucked at the fringe on her chaps. "Is there any way I can get you to leave the ranch for a while?"

He laughed, really laughed and his eyes twinkled like someone enjoying them selves. "Come on, Huffy. Start talking. We can hash this out before getting to the creek."

He made it sound so easy. Sure, life was simple for someone that was bigger and louder than everyone else. He'd never been scared or alone, or without a way out. No, she couldn't trust him.

"I'm not discussing my private life with you." She'd never seen anyone turn to stone before, but his profile could have been chiseled granite.

By the time they arrived at the picnic area, her heart had frozen and thawed several times. He was silent, silent and so far away she probably couldn't have touched him. She didn't dare try.

He parked the truck in the shade of an old oak tree, and got out, walking around to help her out. The sea-green ice of his eyes stunned her, sending waves of unhappiness through her. That was ignorant. She didn't give a hoot what he thought.

She caught her foot in the floor mat, about to take a spill when he grabbed her, pulling her close to his chest.

"Careful, Huffy."

Her cheeks flamed. He was too much to absorb at once. "Thank you."

"Like I said." He touched her chin with his knuckle. "I'll be around."

Her gaze lingered on his long legs and broad shoulders as he sauntered down the grassy slope. He scared her to death, yet she was on fire to lay naked with him in some quiet place, far away.

God, he could read her thoughts, turning to look at her with a lazy smile. "Come on. We're missing all the fun."

She choked squeaky retort. Merely nodded and went to put her hand in his. Yes, this was nightmare and she'd wake up soon. But, not until he stopped gazing at her with his warm green eyes. That proved she was in a dream. He never looked at her with anything but contempt.

It hit her like a hot wind. The jackass was playing her for a fool. Nice one minute, a warthog the next. He was trying to confuse her. Make her vulnerable.

She yanked her hand from his. "I can get there on my own, hillbilly."

"I'm sure you can." He lay his arm across her shoulders. "Don't forget about the bears."

She couldn't help it, looking behind her and to the sides. He gave her what might squeak by as a smile and sauntered off to join the group having a breakfast buffet at a beat-up wooden table.

* * * *

Turk wanted to run. She was staring at him, her blue eyes throwing darts at his ass as he walked away. He'd tried being patient with Huffy. Somehow that never worked. She affected him so deeply and completely, nothing he said or did came out right.

Huffy brought out so many emotions in him, protective, tenderness to ribald humor. She made him feel things he'd never felt and he liked it.

She was so delicate and perfect, he probably would stroke out if she showed the slightest interest in him.

Damn it. He'd settled out here to avoid entanglements and with one flick of her lashes, she'd managed to turn him inside out. He could imagine his eight brothers laughing their ass off at his inability to handle one female.

He'd have plenty to say to brother Gun next time they met. And that might be sooner than either expected. If trouble came in waves, he'd have to get her out of there. Dallas, Texas was just brimming with Gunnison men, and every one of them knew the business end of a forty-five.

The scene at the table took his attention, one that made him grin in spite of his turmoil. Eleven pretty maids lined up at the table where his two ranch hands helped serve them breakfast, gladly dishing up omelets and biscuits.

It didn't seem to matter to the women that the guys were clumsy as two young colts. They all dug in to enjoy the streamside meal. Come to think of it, he was ravenous.

He approached the group, filling a plate with ham and jalapeno pepper omelet and several biscuits and honey. He took two forks before turning to locate Huffy in the group.

She'd taken a seat at the table, pretending to listen to the banter between Conner and several of the women. It looked to him like she was tense as a kitten in a windstorm. She was mentally removed from what went on around her, shoulders rigidly squared and eyes not fixing on anything more than a second or two.

He took a cup of coffee and walked straight to the table. When he took the place beside her, she looked off in the distance.

"I'll share." He placed a fork in her hand and folded her slender fingers around the handle. "As long as you don't eat too much." Like some loser trying to score on a Saturday night, he winked at her. *Oh yeah, Gunnison, you're smooth.*

"Thanks."

He couldn't believe it. She hadn't called him a disgusting pig. He pushed the plate closer to her. "Dig in. I'll get more."

She licked her lips and speared a bite of ham. I am a little hungry."

"Yeah, this air seems to give you an appetite." He handed her a biscuit. "Try this on for size."

The bite she took was ladylike, just enough to feed a bird. Damn, it felt good to be sitting beside her without rocks flying between them. That aggravating guilt feeling stung him in mid-thought.

She was off limits, a wanted man's gun moll for all he knew. *Plus, look at her.* She absolutely had to be too young to be interested in him. He almost chocked on a snort of derision. He didn't know many women that had been around more than sweet faced Huffy. That had sounded jealous and stupid, even to him.

Her blue gaze flitted about, finally lighting on his face while he devoured his second biscuit. "What?" He wiped his mouth. Twice. "Something on my face?"

She laughed and his hands shook. "You're a suspicious man."

He liked the barely visible spray of freckles across her cute nose. He swallowed and condemned himself for the poetic bullshit he was thinking.

Not looking at her was not an easy thing to do. She was sweet smelling, clean and smooth as silk and damn, he wanted her.

His conscience screamed at him, forcing him to think clearly. *Get on your feet clown.*

"I'm going to show you how to cast a line."

He knew no good could come of it, but he would be just doing his job. Taking care of Huffy. "Let's go."

"But, shouldn't we clear the dishes?"

Who the hell was she kidding? He could be sure the woman looking at him with such innocence, had never pulled KP.

"Forget that." He helped her to her feet. "The fish are waiting."

He looked up in time to catch Cole's tomcat grin. The man read him like a book, could see clearly his devious intentions. Turk didn't give a damn.

So what if he was bending his own rules of engagement? No fraternizing with the guests. He shrugged. This was different. He was the boss.

He removed several rods and reels from the back of the truck, explaining how to use the gear. She looked as if she'd taken a step back when he held out an outfit toward her.

He put the rod in her hand, relieved she looked mildly interested and a little afraid of the hooks.

"Okay. I think we have what we need."

It was all he could do to keep from taking her and as they walked. He'd better get his feelings in hand or get her to some safe area. Away from him.

She'd taken on that worried, preoccupied expression again. Proving he wasn't overly stimulating company.

At the water's edge, he tried to start a conversation.

"Ever cast before?" He flicked his line out over the clear water and slowly reeled it in to shore.

He cast out again and observed her from the corner of his eye. Managing fishing gear was foreign to Huffy, quickly earning her disapproval. Turk lay down his rod and reel, taking hers to straighten out the tangled mess she'd made.

"Now, Huffy." He stepped behind her, boxing her in with his arms, taking her hands in his. "Easy. Nice and easy."

She relaxed all right, letting him whip the line out in a perfect arc that settled softly on the gurgling water.

"That's so easy." She pushed him back and struck out on her own.

He tried to grab her arm, but she was quick as a quail, raring back and whipping her arm forward.

"Yowch!" He grabbed his left butt cheek and held the line to keep from being ripped to shreds. "Ease off the rod, Huffy! Put it dowwwwwn!"

She turned to stare at him, shock registering in her eyes. "I...I didn't mean to."

"Step away from the gear, lady."

She meant well, he supposed, but when Huffy ran around to pull what felt like shark's jaws from his backside, he bit down on a yell of pain. "Don't touch my ass!"

"I'm sorry."

He held his hands up as if to ward off evil. "Go get Conner. Now."

She did a stutter-step, and then ran off toward the picnic area. He knew he'd lost his mind when he realized the burning pain in his rump didn't dull his desire for the beautiful woman running to get help.

Lord, Huffy. Why couldn't we have met in a bar somewhere? Just you and me, a few shots of Jack and days and days of sweet, hot lovemaking.

The hooks in his flesh moved and reminded him that he wasn't courting the lady. She'd probably like to take a bite out of him too.

Chapter 8

Abigail ran as fast as she could, crying with some embarrassment and worry. Hooking a person was bad enough, but did it have to be in his rump?

"Help! Conner." She stood at the edge of the crowd, not caring that the women stared at her as if she were sin itself. "Hurry."

Conner trotted to meet her. "What's going on Ma'am?" He looked over her shoulder. "Where's Gunnison?"

"By the stream." She lowered her gaze. "He has a fish hook in his backside."

"A fish hook?" Conner scowled, then laughed. "How the devil did he do that?"

"I don't know." She didn't have to explain to him. "Hurry. He's probably bleeding to death."

Conner shook his head and went to the truck, taking out a first-aide box and some kind of tool from the glove box. "Okay. Let's go save him."

"Hurry. He's in a lot of pain."

"Aw, he's more likely just mad."

Abigail thought she was running fast, but Conner easily passed her, getting to Turk first. Worried about Turk's reaction, she didn't approach him immediately.

She needn't have worried. He didn't look her way once while giving his rendition of what had happened.

"Yeah." He tried to look back at his ass. "She really sank that grappling hook in my hide."

"I'll cut off the lure and then, Gunnison, drop your drawers." Conner took things out of the first aide kit and of course blamed her for the whole thing.

Abigail wanted to see what she'd done. She'd seen men's rears before, and his couldn't be much different.

While Conner was distracted, she moved closer, getting a good look at the damage the hook had done. She cringed when Conner began to cut the steel claws.

She heard the tinny sound of the barbs being cut just before the descent of Turk's jeans to his boot tops.

In her adult relationships with men, she'd never seen such tanned legs or anything so beautifully muscled from thigh to calf. Her awestruck staring shot to the hard bunched glutes of his ass when he yelled in pain.

"Holy fire and Moses! Could you be any faster at that?"

Conner wasn't put off by the outburst, and grinned at her while applying antiseptic to the wound. "He'll be okay."

His amused reassurance did nothing to make her feel better.

"Let me see." Abigail pushed in to stare openmouthed at what she could only see as a life-threatening wound. "Oh my God. I'm sorry. So sorry." She faced Turk with the small bit of courage she possessed. "I'll drive you to the hospital."

He didn't answer immediately, only grimaced while fastening the steel buttons of his jeans. "Don't worry about it. I've got scars that make this look like a hickey."

A hickey! He's making fun of you and you're blushing.

She inhaled to cool her resentment. "At least let me walk you back to the group."

He waved away her offer of help, shaking his head. "You've done enough. Go back with Conner and get the truck. I'll risk you driving me back to the house."

For a man who'd just shown her and the world his naked rear end, he was being pretty high and mighty, talking to her as she were a temperamental child being punished.

She bit back the choice words that probably would have burned his ears. He barked a final command when she turned to leave.

"Conner will walk with you." He grimaced and rubbed his backside.

"I don't need Conner. I know where the truck is." What was his problem now?

"I said he'd go with you."

Abigail denied herself the pleasure of torpedoing him where he stood. No use provoking the beast further.

"Shall we, Conner. The bear needs to be alone."

Getting back to the picnic area was easy, but shifting the truck in gear was another story. How many gears did it have? The thing bucked and lurched, roaring like an angry dragon as she forced it to back up, turn and move down the hill toward its master.

The brake and gas pedal were a real stretch for her to work correctly. He'd seemed perfectly comfortable driving the huge beast. Her stomach was in cold knots by the time she arrived back where he waited. Naturally he stood, hands on hips, glaring at her as she ground the gears and chewed her lip.

He looked to heaven with a scowl dark enough to hide the sun before opening the door to climb into the passenger's seat. "Well, let's go. You do drive don't you?"

The moment had arrived on hot winds of pent up anger and hurt feelings. Abigail gripped the steering wheel and ground the gears with no concern about his angry glare. The man had to learn she would never accept his crude disrespect.

She was bursting with euphoria when the gears meshed and the truck shot forward, spitting dirt and rocks behind them as she pressed the accelerator down to the floor.

"Slow down! Your driving sucks!"

"I'm fine! Don't worry about me." Her glance in his direction revealed a pleasing sight. He gripped the windshield frame as if it were a life raft.

"I'm not worried about you, damn it! Stop the damn truck."

"In time, you horses ass. In time."

Rocks, trees and startled deer were a blur as she took Turk on the ride of his life. Of course there would be hell to pay if she didn't kill them both, but it was too delightful to stop just yet.

The ranch house loomed in the distance as she slid around a curve, frantically turning the steering wheel to right the huge gas hog.

She romped on the brake pedal, stopping the truck with a great show of lurching, screeching and gear grinding. He moved over to open her door and confiscate the truck.

"Get out."

"When I'm good and ready, you redneck-bully."

He stared at her for a moment, a glint of disbelief in his eyes. She steeled herself for the tirade that was certainly coming.

No way was he going to win this scuffle with her running away and hiding. She grabbed the keys and dropped them down the front of her halter-top. The cool metal was a shocking delight against her breast.

"Let me see now. You think I won't know how to fish for those." He eyed her with cool speculation.

"You can try."

He exhaled as if she were the most wearisome annoyance in the world. "Typical. What are you hoping to get with this little episode? Didn't you get enough attention from your grandfather?"

It was no accident he'd used the term, grandfather. Turk never did anything accidentally.

"Okay. So you checked on my background when I booked here. That is none of your business."

"Wrong again." His mouth set in a hard line of anger. "Now, hand over those keys before I strip you naked as a jaybird."

"Such a gentleman." She waved her hand and lifted her chin to add haughtiness to her comment. "I of course saw your genteel qualities right off."

"Knock it off, Huffy. You need to can the finishing school shit and grow up. The keys!"

"Go to hell."

He was quick, jerking her to his chest, then plopping her down on the seat. Surprised but undaunted, Abigail kicked and screamed, liking his hard glare of distaste.

Still reeling from being tossed onto her back, she stared wide-eyed as he leaned over to push his face close to hers.

"I hear you like the rough guys." He hardly reacted to her bite to his arm. "Sorry gal, but I don't beat my women or horse fuck them." He smacked her ass and pulled her to an upright position. "Don't confuse me with your pussy boyfriends."

"That you could be mistaken as any friend of mine is laughable. They are, first of all, human, and men that walk upright." Her voice shook, but her words were razor sharp. "You're saying things that tell me you have a lot of bad information about me. And, even if it were accurate, I fail to see how it is any of your concern."

The anger on his face evaporated into cold disgust. "You're dead wrong, Huffy. All those wild adventures you've gone on have caught up with you. I don't give a tinker's damn what you did before you slid in to my space." He paused as if he were reviewing her past. "I'd never look at you twice under normal circumstances, but you and your wrong headed boyfriend have invaded my life. Nothing would make me happier if you'd never blown in here with your snotty ways and little girl tantrums. You're not my type, so don't ever think I'd have felt differently in any scenario."

"I'm not good enough for the smelly cowboy?" She arched her brows and smirked with what she thought could be interoperated as balls. His fingers tightened on her arm. "You're hurting me. Do you get a riser doing things like that?"

"You've never been hurt." Pissed off barely covered his expression or his voice. "Get this straight. I have to keep you here, not because I like you, but because your latest Don Juan has made you an accomplice in his game of espionage." He let her go, forgetting the keys apparently. "And one more thing. Don't worry about giving me a riser. Never happen because of you."

Chapter 9

Abigail sat in quiet reflection of Turk's ugly description of her life. He'd cut her to the quick and she still hurt. She couldn't believe there were tears burning her cheeks.

Crying wasn't something she allowed herself. Not in years. Her mother had said it often, and Abigail believed it. *Weak women cry. Smart women leave.*

Facing Turk's angry speech confirmed the truth. Had her bid for independence been genuine or an idiot's daydream?

Past memories of her home life slipped into her thoughts. The angry, shouting episodes between her beautiful mother and angrier, impassioned grandfather rose, vivid and frightening. Until now, she'd put all the reasons for the battles far from her mind.

She couldn't banish the scene of Christmas ten years earlier. How could she forget her mother, moving around the Christmas tree, grabbing up gift-wrapped boxes and throwing them into the fireplace. Abigail saw clearly a swarthy, grinning man in the doorway, his car keys jingling as he watched the family feud.

Her grandfather shouted that she was to leave with nothing, not even his granddaughter. Funny, Abigail hadn't ever let the scene play out until today. Her screams for Momma to take her were ignored and Francesca Monica Van Huffington swept from the huge, brick estate without looking back.

All right, so her mother had deserted her. So what? Her grandfather had tried to browbeat her into his idea of perfection and hated her for standing up to him.

Abigail didn't want to remember any of that. There was another issue she'd come upon when she was a senior in high school. She'd pretended for years her mother was simply too chic to take a husband's name when she married. How naïve could she have been?

After that, her link to a sane world had been through her lovely grandmother, Monica Regina Montega. Their time together had been rare, two weeks in the winter and a month in summer. Her grandfather's wealth and connections stopped any attempt by her grandmother to take her permanently.

Finally after much soul searching, she'd asked her grandfather why her mother had kept her maiden name. He flew into a rage and suffered a heart attack, but not before telling her the truth about her supposedly immoral mother. He'd called her mother a tamp that never married and Abigail was a bastard by a New York dandy who hadn't wanted a family.

From that day on, Abigail defied intervention from the world, especially her grandfather. The beginning of her search for a relationship began with Ethan Trueblood, the detective in Dallas that had taken her from a brawl in a five-star hotel in Dallas. Ethan was barely an adult himself and they found instant happiness in one another.

Mixed in there was Josh Ross from Amarillo, her bull rider with those bowlegs. Abigail smiled just thinking of him. He was too young in her opinion, but his sweet smile and soft-spoken ways touched her heart and they'd become lovers while he was on the circuit. The relationship ended when he made up with his ex-girlfriend and decided to stay on the family ranch.

Abigail hated thinking about her past, her cold family and her own selfish ways. The only thing she had plenty of was money. She spent it as quickly as it was deposited into her checking account, buying lavish clothing and gifts for her friends.

A lot of it went to her last romantic entanglement, Brick Highlander, a premiere forward for the Dallas Stars. He was a prick, but so good-looking and sexy, she had to have him.

A Bostonian to the bone, Brick refused to buy property in Dallas, going back to Boston as often as possible. They'd stayed together in her apartment for one season, their noisy union ending after he brought home two women with plans to have a four way. He told her she would be in the middle of the knot. She called her ex, the detective, and he happily evicted Brick and his lady friends from her apartment.

She wished now she'd been a little more frugal, instead of being stranded with a man who despised her.

Her deep sigh reflected her dread of going to the house to face Turk. All she wanted now was to escape. Hopefully he wouldn't be in the commons room.

She got out of the truck, walked quickly to the house, and then stopped at the front door. Although apprehensive, she opened the screen-door and stepped inside, pausing to collect her thoughts.

The house hummed with the charged silence of recent laughter and conversation. Now it was softly quiet, the pale afternoon light lending the house a sweetness and yet a lonely feeling.

Stop being a fool. You've become a real coward and it has to stop.

Her legs felt as heavy as lead weights as she climbed the stairs to her room. Escaping into sleep was the most pressing thing on her mind. She'd left the blinds down and the room was cool and dimly lit.

She yawned, stripping as she went into the bathroom to start the shower. The perfect water beat on her tense shoulders like tiny fingers.

The warmth and pleasant massage woke her sensuous nature, taking her into the pulsing world of erotic delights where she bid Turk to join her. As if it happened everyday, Turk came to her, naked and warm, his body sleek and toned under her caressing hands. So many things to explore, to clasp her fingers around and ways to pull him closer. His usual stormy observation softened as he gazed into her eyes with uninhibited desire, his wonderful mouth smiling at her.

Caught up in the sweetness of being in his favor, she plummeted into the misty world of sexual fantasy, enjoying his hard body pressing her to the wall to touch her swollen folds. She moved her hips against his fingers that stroked and babied her clit, then pushed deep inside to bring her to a rapid, pyrotechnical climax, leaving her weak and shaken.

After the quake had subsided, she didn't spend time analyzing what had occurred. She was simply horny and Turk kept sex on her mind. End of story.

She turned off the shower and stood naked in the bedroom door, looking at something propped against her pillows.

Curiosity drew her to the bed where she stared in confusion at the cell phone pressed to her pillow. Turk had brought this phone, had been in her room. But, it didn't belong to her. Maybe this was one more of his unsubtle ways of telling her to get out.

Okay, this had to be met head on. Her pulse raced while she dressed, fingers shaking too badly to button slacks or every tiny button on a blouse. She grabbed the easiest thing to get on, a peasant blouse and a prairie skirt with an elastic waist. Digging in the bottom of her trunk, she found a pair of fawn moccasins and jammed her feet into them.

She was clumsy with a fear that came back to haunt her from years past. The sounds of hoots and whistles had dimmed some in her mind, but she still recalled the panic in her heart. A gang of boys had followed her home from the movies one night and she wouldn't leave the house for days afterward. There was the same feeling in the house and she wanted to flee like she had then.

There wasn't time to fiddle with her hair, so she twisted it into a loose coil at her nape as she headed downstairs to find Turk.

The house was still completely deserted, the feeling of being watched hitting her.

Where could he have gone? The hearth room greeted her with a quiet sullenness, or was that her imagination? Something different hovered in the warm air of the house and it frightened her.

Never one to believe in the unseen things most of her friends talked about, Abigail didn't like whatever pursued her. Practically running, she crossed the oak plank floor to look out the window. Nothing to worry about. The colorful bed of Zinnia hadn't been disturbed, and still nodded prettily in the breeze.

Looking past the flowerbed and the white glider on the shady patio, she noticed something fluttering on the stable door. Cornflower blue. Turk's shirt.

Mad at her or not, Abigail had to be with him right now. Something frightening had arrived in Lone Horse and she didn't want to know what it was or face it alone.

Her feet barely touched the ground as she hurried across the yard and along the brick pathway to the stable doors, all the while resisting the temptation to look back, absolutely sure something was chasing her. She was gasping for breath when her hands finally locked on the big, copper door latch of the heavy door. Chiding herself for such cowardice, she took a moment to peer around the door, making sure he was there.

"Huffy. That you?"

Her heart pumped fiercely at the sound of his rich baritone. What could she say? I'm a baby? I'm scared?

"Huffy, in here."

She followed his voice, halting when he quit whatever he was doing to glance up at her.

She licked her lips and tugged on her skirt. "I was just looking for you."

He went back to working saddle soap on an old, worn looking saddle. "You were?"

"Yes." Why didn't he lay into her? That would be much better than ignoring her. "I found what you left in my room."

That got his attention. "What I left? What are you talking about?" He stopped what he was doing and came around the saddle rail to stand close to her.

"You left this in my room, on my bed. It was nice of you, but it isn't mine." An invisible force, his scent and warmth snapping a lead line on her emotions drew her to him.

"Let me see that." His voice was free of anger and disgust as he held his hand out to take the phone. "This isn't one of yours?"

"No. You took the battery from both my phones. This isn't mine."

He quickly moved her inside the first stall. "Anything else different in the house?"

Should she tell him about the eerie sense of foreboding? No, he'd scoff at her. "Just unusually quiet. I took a shower before I noticed this on my bed."

He moved her to the rear of the small enclosure, opening the phone to flip the batteries out. "Huffy, I want you to stay close to me from now on. This phone says we had company while we were out. He's coming back."

"But, I don't understand."

"Just listen to me. I don't know how this all stacks up, but that guy you're waiting for is in a truckload of trouble. He may not know it, but he's gotten you entangled in the mess."

"Shane?" She stared at him in disbelief. "He's harmless, a big braggart. He's a baby and wouldn't hurt me or anyone else."

"Maybe...but right now you have a man determined to get what he wants, even if he has to kill you to get it. I expect you to do what I tell you and keep quiet!"

"You're quite sure I'll just stand here and shuffle my feet, waiting for your next command."

He scowled at her before yanking the saddle off the rail. "You don't have a choice." Handling the saddle with one hand, Turk hadn't run out of bad things to say about her friend. "Look, he's being used like a three dollar mule by another malcontent bent on hurting a lot of people. His buddy wouldn't mind killing both of you."

He was shouting at her, and it dredged up all the horror of her childhood. Backing up against the stall, she forced her lips to move and tears to flee.

"You're a despicable person. I'll do anything to get away from you."

* * * *

Turk knew she was staring at him where he folded saddle blankets, probably picking just the right spot to sink an ice pick.

"When do you think he'll show up here?"

"What?"

He took a second to study her beautiful face. Nothing in the world ever took his fancy like Huffy.

She was holding up damn well under the heat he'd given her. She didn't whine or make excuses and she didn't shirk on her workload. The best thing about her was that she didn't try to use sex on him. She was damn fine.

"Your boyfriend. Remember him?" He couldn't believe how torn he was at that moment. Kiss her or just strap her to his side. She was neck deep in trouble and didn't know it.

Damn it, Gunnison. She's not a recruit. She's a woman, one that requires a gentler hand. If you can pull that off.

"What I'm trying to say is someone is leaving messages to scare you."

She glanced over her shoulder. "I'm scared, but its not Shane doing this. He's bringing money so I can escape."

"Escape? From what? To where?" He resented the fact she wanted to run from him, escape with another man. "Let's say he's lucky enough to make it here with the FBI and an enemy of the government on his skinny ass. You're not leaving with him."

She bristled instantly. "You and your kind are what I'm trying to get away from. And, if I have to die trying, I shall."

The emotion in her words stunned Turk, and rubbed his male nerves the wrong way. "Want me to draw pictures of the ways the guy chasing him can make you scream before he kills you? He thinks you know all about this damned scheme and won't hesitate to cut your throat."

"I don't believe you. I haven't done anything."

"Aw hell." Turk was getting riled with her inability to get the picture. "See, if this Shane you're involved with doesn't have what Kufu Rama Fa wants, he'll be pretty sure he gave it to you. In any case, he's not going to let you skip away from this. Understand?"

Turk didn't like speaking to her as if she was stupid, but she forced him. The flush of pink on her cheeks was resentment, not timidity.

"Stop talking about Shane as if he were less worthy than a virus. He's the only friend I have and I'm worried about him."

Turk could see that, and he envied the punk. No woman ever gave a rat's ass how he fared.

"Okay. Don't start crying yet. Maybe we can keep his hide in one piece." Touching her cheek, he allowed his voice to soften. "Right now, I'm more concerned about yours."

She ducked her chin, and her voice shook as she spoke. "No need. I'm not afraid."

"Learn to be. It won't be as dangerous while the other women are here, but after they leave, you can't step out of the house without me."

"Leave." She gazed at him, fear and worry in her eyes. "When are they leaving?"

"This coming Saturday. Conner will be driving them to the airport." He inhaled deeply to defuse the large jolt of nerves pelting his gut, trying to digest the thought she'd be with him for a while longer. "The lodge is closing until December."

"But...I have nowhere to go until Shane gets here."

Turk understood he'd never sleep again until he had some clue to this woman's desires. "This Shane. He's really important to you?" God, he hoped not.

Stepping outside to yank his shirt from the hook it hung on, he wanted to slug the lucky boy named Shane, while listening to Huffy speak of him.

"I love Shane. He's my lifeline to an existence out of hell."

Well, Gunnison. You can't compete with that.

Chapter 10

Abigail believed Turk had been telling the truth, but hated his mean perception of Shane. Right now, Turk ignored her, buttoning his shirt and stuffing the tail in his pants. He winced after accidentally hitting his wound.

She avoided eye contact until he finished.

Without a word, he took her hand and led her to the door, looking around before putting on his hat. He seemed to be caught in a dilemma, glancing at her and then the empty gun rack over the door.

"How fast can you run, Huffy?"

She hadn't been worried before, but he'd changed her mind with his attitude. It was foolish, but she bragged on her athletic ability. "Actually, I can fly."

"Spread your wings, Tinker Bell." He seemed to never be without one of those silly names to call her. "Aim for the back door."

"Okay." She breathed deep, remembering her days on the track team at school. Feeling his hand take hers was a definite plus and reassurance.

Running beside Turk was an eye-opener, reminding her how slow her time had been. She wasn't fast or fleet of foot, the proof jumping up in her face when she tripped in a small depression. She spread her arms instead of wings, feeling certain her face would scrub the rough trail when she landed. Turk caught her around the waist and carried her on his hip as he blazed a trail for the house.

He let her down when he reached the patio.

At the back door, he gripped her arm until she thought it would break while he yanked open the screen and pulled her into the mudroom. He shut the door and locked it, looking out the etched glass window.

Her imagination ran wild along with her heartbeat. "Was that necessary?"

"Until I load my weapon, it is."

There he went again. "A gun!"

He strode toward his office, and from the side view she got of his face, he was laughing. He looked around the door and hid whatever he was doing, the sound of metal clinking and clacking much like a door being locked.

She eyed him with renewed fear as he walked across the hall to take her hand. "What's so funny? I don't like guns."

"I want you to stop calling this a gun." He touched the huge thing stuffed in his waistband. "It's a weapon, better known as a Glock22."

Abigail fought the desperation that twisted her heart. "You're not going to hurt Shane, are you? I won't let you."

His expression was new to her, puzzled and ...she couldn't read it. He must be angry, his gaze no longer bearing any sign of mirth. He frightened her when he became distant, cold as ice and biting with his remarks.

"Huffy, you can stay in your room. I'll keep watch downstairs until the other women check out. After that, I'll set up outside your door."

Something had changed his mind. He no longer wanted to be near her. "Okay."

"Okay, what?"

"I want to go up to my room."

"Not until I check it out."

She jumped when he turned at the foot of the stairs to scowl at her. "Let's go."

Her slow reaction obviously didn't please him, his hand shooting out to grip her arm. "I don't like being roughed up."

He released her, muttering something that sounded like an apology.

She followed him inside the small room she called home, leaning against the wall while he moved around, bumping into things. He checked the bathroom, the closet, and finally under the bed. He pulled the white curtains aside and looked out the window, eyeing the small overhang beneath.

"All clear. I'll see you downstairs at supper."

Abigail spent the rest of the afternoon in dejected misery, lying on her bed. Consumed in angry self-reproach, she tossed one more crumpled sheet of paper onto the floor. The more she calculated the amount of money she needed, the more frightened she became. What if Shane couldn't bring enough cash to get her out of the country?

Poor Shane. Poor her. Rolling onto her stomach, she looked out the window to watch Conner and Luke removing the horse's harnesses to lead them to the stable. The scene could have been from Farm & Home, until Turk showed up.

She was free to observe him without the usual fear he'd catch her looking, and see her vulnerability. Her gaze was gentle, touching him like a soft kiss. He had a wondrous face with all its sharp plains and chiseled features.

Turk mystified her, standing tall and proud with his delicious secrets hidden. The heady memory of the scent he wore sent a warm quickening through her body.

There brewed in her heart a worrisome mixture of desire and anger toward Turk, pulling her in crazy directions.

Crawling from the bed, she sat on the windowsill to see the object of her discontent more clearly. His well-made hands held her attention, calling back their imagined time together in her shower. The flash of desire blooming through Abigail shook her to her toes, making her grab for the window curtain to stop a certain fall.

Sinking slowly to the floor, she sat in stunned silence, revelation gripping her pounding heart. She had deep, torrid feelings for Turk. To her surprise, a swift river of gentle, caring emotion coursed through her blood as well. She'd never felt like that about anyone before.

The truth was painful, bringing tears to her eyes and an ache that would haunt her for the rest of her life. Why did she have to feel anything for him? He found her repulsive and completely without feminine qualities.

Worse, she was uncertain of her friend's safety if Turk found him on his property. There was only one choice to make. Make it to Puerto Vallarta any way she could.

Tears fell unnoticed until she heard someone knocking on her door.

Hurry, you never let anyone see you cry.

Using the tail of her blouse, she dried her eyes. "Who is it?"

"Santa Claus."

It was him! And she must look horrible. "Just a minute." She jumped up and ran to her dressing table. It was covered with cosmetics bottles and hair rollers, the room a tumbled mess with clothing scattered everywhere. She wiped mascara from her cheeks and whipped a brush through her hair. It made no difference. He wouldn't see it anyway. "Come in."

Turk opened the door and looked inside, his gaze flicking over the cluttered mess. "It's supper time." She was devastated by his quick grimace of apparent disgust when his stare swept over a pair of her pink silk panties. "We're having strawberry ice cream." He licked his lips. "And angel food cake. Cookie told me to tell you."

"Oh." What was she supposed to do now? He rubbed his jaw and glanced at her bed. A hot blush colored her face. "I'll be down in a minute."

"We're all eating in the kitchen tonight." Looking like a cornered tiger, he backed out the door. "Hustle it up."

She listened to his retreating footsteps on the stairs, her thoughts quickly going over ways to slip out of the house without detection.

With her face scrubbed clean and a desire to just get away from Lone Horse, Abigail gathered her nerves into a knot and went down to the noisy kitchen.

The meal was being served buffet style in the huge old kitchen. The room made Abigail think of a favorite picture book from years gone by. The wall-sized brick fireplace near the back door reminded her of the Christmases she had foolishly dreamed of.

White cabinets and colorful tiled counters warmed the room, along with the glass-fronted dish shelves. Fresh fruit and vegetables were piled high in glass bowls and wire baskets.

She looked up, hearing her name being called over the chatter going on.

It was Cookie, overseeing the whole thing. She was a cherry-faced woman with a kind smile and snow white hair. She waved a wooden spoon in the air to get Abigail's attention.

"I have a warm plate for you, Abigail. Here." She handed her a large dinner plate filled with fries and a mammoth sized burger, not to mention big slices of onion and pickles. "Sit down over there by Mister Gunnison."

Abigail darted a glance at Turk. She'd never heard him addressed by his last name. "Well, if he wouldn't mind being crowded."

Cookie howled with laughter. "Honey, he's lonesome if there ain't a dozen people elbowing him at the table."

"Because he was in the Army?"

Cookie laughed heartily again. "You could say that. He's used to eating meals with eight brothers."

A smile crept over Abigail's lips, the idea of how joyful his life must have been as a child warmed her heart.

After a reassuring nod from Cookie, she edged closer to the table, waiting for Turk to notice her. "Do you have room for me?" Of all things, her voice broke and her hands shook. She was nervous around him, afraid of looking like a fool.

He glanced up, still chewing a bite of his burger, and wiped his mouth. "Sure." He pulled out one of the heavy oak chairs. "There's plenty of room."

Once he'd poured her a glass of iced tea, and handed her the ketchup, he went back to eating his meal.

Abigail couldn't imagine a family of that size and all male to boot. Curiosity made her tread on dangerous territory. His personal life. "Did you have fun with your brothers?"

"Huh?" He leveled his turquoise gaze on her for several long seconds, and then laughed. "Yeah, every day was a fairytale."

She looked down at her plate, wondering how she could have been so naïve. "You're making fun of me."

"Naw," he said, chuckling over some secret thought. "You don't have fun with eight brothers. You have skirmishes." He eyed her with a half smile. "How about you, Huffy? Any brothers or sisters?"

"No." Understanding the loneliness without siblings. It seemed to her Turk had more than his share and didn't appreciate them.

He quizzed her now like a cop, suspicion in his eyes. She regretted ever speaking to him.

Bertha and several other women had stopped eating to eavesdrop on their conversation.

Abigail found a thread of courage and took up the subject again. "There are eight more like you?"

"Not like me, but almost as good." He glanced at her plate. "You'd better eat up. I'm not much of a cook."

"You don't need to concern yourself with cooking."

Fool! He's looking at you with that searching glint in his eyes.

"You planning on dining elsewhere, Huffy?"

"Absolutely." She decided to go with it, pretend ignorance to his meaning. "Just as soon as possible."

Accomplishing that took the last ounce of calm she possessed. The heat of his calculating stare branded her with its deep probe. She'd probably given off some female scent only an animal like Turk recognized as pre-escape aroma. Hopefully, it covered the scent of arousal that began to stir under his quiet observation.

Bertha finally wearied of their conversation and left the table. She had packing to finish, like everyone except Abigail. The thought of being alone with Turk fortified her determination to leave the lodge.

She pushed her plate away and stood. "Excuse me."

"You haven't had your ice cream."

"You eat it." She dropped her napkin on the table. "I have some laundry."

He touched her wrist, his eyes narrowed as he spoke quietly. "We'll try to not wake you in the morning." Sweet fire leapt from his fingers trailing across her knuckles. "Sleep in if you want."

Fear of reacting positively to any suggestion from him speared her heart.

"I don't need your okay to do anything. How long or where I sleep is no concern of yours." She pulled her hand from his reach, and concluded her icy reply. "Make all the noise you want. I don't pay that much attention to where you may be."

Surely, he noticed her stiff walk and trembling shoulders. She made it to the door, glancing back to find Turk following her with a stare that would dissect an insect.

Getting away from Lone Horse didn't mean she'd ever escape those exotic eyes.

Chapter 11

There was definitely something different about Huffy's attitude tonight, but Turk didn't have time to figure it out. Nailing things down for the next three-month's closing occupied his mind.

In the morning, the house would be quiet again. Instead of twelve women to look after, there would be one. Huffy.

He stayed at the table while the kitchen and dining room cleared out. Even Cookie fell silent, probably anxious to finish cleaning the kitchen.

He took his dishes to the sink and rinsed them, placing them in one of the commercial-sized dishwashers. Cookie broke the silence, chattering happily about her plans for a long vacation. Her face turned another shade of pink when he handed her a check.

"What's that for?" She swiped at her white hair. "But thank you. Not many know it, but you're a good man."

"Never mind the compliments, Cookie." He patted her shoulder. "Buy the kids something fun."

"Yesiree." She dried her hands on her apron. "Got a ticket to fly back to Dallas. I can't wait to see all my grandbabies."

Turk liked the way she placed her grandkids pictures with his all over the house. "Have fun, Cookie, but don't forget I need you back here in three months."

"Don't worry, Mister Gunnison. I know you can't handle all this alone." Her cherub face lit up in a sweet smile.

They chatted a few more minutes until she began closing the shades and hanging up tea towels. Turk took the fresh hermit cookie she offered and took a hefty bite.

"Okay, Cookie. I'll see you back here in December." He walked to the door. "Have a nice time." He was going to have a hell of a time getting out of the house tonight if he had to keep chatting with everyone. He was wasting precious minutes and he had a limited window of

She waved and went back to shutting drawers and hanging up her apron, after stuffing a hefty vacation bonus from him in her dress pocket.

Conner and Luke were going trout fishing up in the mountains early in the morning. He would have to bribe Conner into one more favor before everyone cleared out.

There was a hot shower and a hotter woman waiting at Blue Bear's Balls Emporium. His step got lighter at the thought of being clamped between Glenda Fowler's nice thighs. The thought jabbed his nerves with hot need.

Glenda was a woman left behind by a trucker husband with little to call her own. Except her desire to have fun. She stayed at Blue Bear's Ball's, living in the small cottage behind the place and serving beer as a job. Turk liked her. Glenda was the one a man talked to when he was a little lonely, or wanted to be in a woman's company. Out here, she was a precious commodity.

Turk walked quickly to the hearth room where Conner was locking windows and lowering shades.

"Hey, Conner." Turk made his request while unbuttoning his shirt. "How about sticking around another couple hours. I'll pay time and a half."

"Blue Bear's, huh?" Conner knew where he was going, and why.

"Yeah, like you haven't been there six times in the past two weeks."

Conner nodded. "Okay. I'll do it, since I'm leaving tomorrow." He lowered his voice. "Are you nuts? What's wrong with Abigail?"

She doesn't figure into this conversation." Turk glanced toward the stairs. "You just make sure you keep trouble out while I'm gone."

Conner saluted him in a cocky show of drama, clicking his heels to add to the drama. "Not to worry. She's as safe as a babe in swaddling clothes."

"See that she stays that way." Turk headed for his quarters. "I'm outta here."

His shower was fast and exhilarating, priming his appetite for what waited for him. Fast and hot would be fine with him, no long courtship or prolonged foreplay. Glenda liked to fuck and wanted it quick.

He still had beads of water on his skin when he pulled on fresh clothes. Desire for female company made him clumsy.

The hot streak gripping his nuts carried his thoughts to the softly scented beauty just a few feet above.

Was she sleeping?

Probably mad and pouting.

He grimaced against the pain of urges, so confused, his blood had to be flowing backward. What was wrong with him? Foaming at the mouth over a woman who saw him as a backwoods clod. Here he was, wanting to get on her good side to hear just a few words of praise. God help him if she ever just hinted she might want him.

He steadied his fingers enough to stuff in his shirttail and button his jeans, glancing up at the ceiling. In his haste to get to Glenda's waiting thighs, he collided with Old Calijah, the wooden, cigar store Indian that kept vigil by the door.

The thing hit the floor with a boom, rocking back and forth on the oak planks.

"Damn it!"

If she hadn't been awake, she was now.

He shoved his wallet into his back pocket, careful not to use the side still throbbing from the earlier hooking. In a hurry, he grabbed his hat and struck out for the door, into the especially fragrant night air.

He liked the jingle of his keys as he hurried to the truck. The sound meant he was going to town. In Gunnison lingo, that meant, going to get some.

The truck was cool and clean, an invigorating change from the dusty heat of chasing runaway horses, being snagged like a carp and a woman that hated him.

Damn the truck smelled good.

Grabbing a cigar from the glove box, he lit it, looking in the rearview mirror for a second. Things didn't feel just right tonight, too quiet, too good smelling. The scent was familiar, intoxicating and probably all in his mind. Then he remembered Huffy had been in the truck earlier. He wondered if he'd ever forget her perfume.

Slamming the Ram into gear, he drove out of view of his house, wanting to leave that woman's tempting memory behind. Glenda would be happy to see him and not expect after talk or a reservation for a repeat.

Even though it was chilly, he rolled down the window to blow the tormenting scent out of his nostrils. On the plus side, the freezing temperature roused his blood and chased the cobwebs from his head.

Twenty minutes later, he was pulling up in front of Blue Bear's. The jolt of pain in his ass when he jumped out of the truck cooled his ardor a bit. He looked around before rubbing the throbbing wound, and hurried inside the weathered log establishment.

* * * *

Abigail shivered with the cold, hugging her arms around herself for warmth. Between the frigid air and cigar smoke, she had considered letting Turk know she was squashed on the floor behind his seat.

Thankfully, he'd reached his destination before she died from the elements. After a few minutes, she crawled from the cramped space and out of the truck. She'd seen this place once before. They'd driven past it on her first day at the lodge.

It wasn't much to look at, certainly not a spa or vacation inn. That made no difference to her now. There was a sign stating a public phone was inside. She'd taken change from the phone table and didn't feel a bit guilty about it.

Before opening the frosted, glass-paneled door, she tried to peek inside to check the place out. Nothing. The windows were blocked. That meant she had to sneak in, and risk being seen by Turk.

Luckily, a couple staggered out, laughing and hugging, paying no attention when she slipped by as they left.

The place smelled of saddles and horse feed, but the overriding smell was beer.

Abigail waited until her eyes adjusted to the dim light before skirting stacks of feed sacks and barrels of apples. She took one and moved toward the sign blinking above a telephone booth a few feet away.

Before she went inside the small glassed-in booth, she checked out the tiny dance floor where several couples lurched around to a country western tune. Across the room was a bar loaded with beer bottles and pickled eggs.

She shuddered and took in the whole scene of cowboys and eager women who didn't seem to care where the boys put their hands.

Remembering why she had stowed away, she eyed the cold drink machine. She could use something refreshing while making her call to Shane.

She dug in her slacks pocket for change, glancing up when a woman at the bar shrieked playfully.

"Turk! You stop that!"

Abigail's head jerked up and her ears burned, hearing his rich full laugh. What was he doing? He should be drinking a beer like the rest of the hillbillies, not making a woman scream with pleasure.

Curiosity pulled her from the shadows to better see what was going on.

She searched out the source of the giggling laughter, her gaze locking on the couple at the end of the bar.

Turk and a hefty woman in a thigh high leather mini were glued together in the juncture of his legs. His hands were plastered to her round hips, his knee splitting her thighs.

He was kissing her neck!

Anger blazed through her while he patted that woman's round buns. Bloody hell. He never so much as gave her a tumble, and this one was getting all he had.

She didn't know why she reacted so strongly, but the feeling hit hard and left an ache in her heart. He was in her line of vision and she could see his eyes were half closed, his smile seductive.

Somehow, he must have felt her furious glare, because he looked across the room to spear her with a cold stare.

There was no escape. Abigail couldn't make her feet move, before Turk put the woman aside to stride across the dance floor toward her.

One thing she could see was the anger burning in his eyes. He didn't speak to her, simply reached out to take her arm.

Abigail pulled back, almost scooting on the sawdust-covered floor before she screamed at him. "Take your hands off me, damn you!"

"Quiet down, Huffy." He pulled her up against him. "How did you slip past Conner?"

She slapped his arm. "Didn't have to."

"I forgot how clever you are. Did you give any thought to that freak who could be hanging around here, just looking for the chance to drag you off to the woods."

She stared at him before snorting with derision. "Yes, I'm in so much danger you had time to sneak off to get laid."

The look in his eyes said she had made him angrier, and he grabbed her hand. "Give that to me."

"What? I hate you."

"I don't give a shit." He tried to grab her flailing arm. "I said, give it to me."

She couldn't clench her fist against the shaking he was giving it, and coins clattered around them, rolling onto the dance floor.

After glaring at her for a second, he pulled her out the door and hurried to the truck. She could feel the heat from his body as she bumped against him. His aftershave warmed her blood to a sizzle and her libido stormed through her body. She thought she might faint. Her emotions went on a wild tumble, her head spun and her knees threatened to buckle.

Out in the chilly air, their breaths mingled like warm mists. He led her to the truck, yanking the door open to boost her up into the seat, climbing in with her in a silent rage.

"You'd better start taking this seriously, Pandora!" He looked in the rearview mirror. "What were you doing in Blue Balls?"

"None of your affair. You're just mad because I messed up your hot date." She crossed her arms over her breasts and sniffed. "My God, you're a disgusting pig."

He didn't comment, simply glanced at her.

She flicked a careless hand at him. "So, this is where you come for sex. Sickening."

Too late she realized she'd gone too far. He dragged her across the cold, leather seat to push his face so close to hers, his lips brushed hers as he berated her.

"Don't say another word, or you'll be taking her place." He grabbed his crotch in a suggestive way. "Not another word."

"If you're trying to scare me, you've failed miserably."

Jabbing his finger in her direction, he issued another warning. "What did I say about talking?"

The truck roared and plowed through the cold mist while Turk hit the steering wheel and threw her coin purse out the window.

She smiled secretively, aware now that she could push his all mighty buttons. "Close the window. I'm tired of freezing."

He looked her way with a sardonic smile. "I can fix that before you can spit."

Chapter 12

Turk couldn't believe his eyes when he'd spotted Huffy glaring across the dance floor at him back at Blue Bear's Balls. At first, he figured he was fantasizing about her, but her snooty little scowl of disapproval had broken his bubble of let's pretend.

He immediately thought Conner hadn't been watching his post and let her slip out of the house. He'd gone to the head and left her unguarded. Hell no, it wasn't Conner's fault. He was probably still propped up against her door, wishing he'd finish up early with Glenda.

Damn. He'd been mere inches from hard riding bliss when Huffy ruined it. Now, she sat calm as a kitten, occasionally glancing his way as if she couldn't believe what a pig he was.

His attention quickly shifted to a huge rock that had tumbled free from the hillside and rolled onto the road. It hadn't been there when he drove to Blue Bear's. Slowing to look around, he sniffed the air for the smell of a trap. This was too dumb and way too hard for a city slicker to pull off. He steered around it, hitting the gas for a fast getaway. The tires spun and the truck swerved back onto the gravel road. Maybe he was becoming too suspicious.

She gasped and grabbed his arm, not yelling like a typical female, but leaning forward as if she was excited. The woman liked danger if she held the reins. He remembered the wild ride she'd taken him on.

He had to admit he liked the thrill of being a little wild, being in control of the situation. It reminded him of ramming through enemy lines with live ammo exploding around him.

As expected, she screwed the moment up with a lame threat.

"You just get me home and I won't report you to the authorities."

He nodded toward the door. "You want to walk the rest of the way back to the lodge?"

She looked out at the deep purple night, not altering her attitude a hell of a lot. "I'm not afraid, just cold."

Damn she's a hard head.

Huffy had no concept of real danger. He'd known when their eyes met for the first time, she was from money, but lived a dangerous, no love, no holds barred life. No one had to tell him. She had a haunted aura about her.

Right now, the little snip that seemed hell bent on making his life miserable looked cold and he wouldn't be mean. Even if she had ruined his night. She hunkered down, hugging herself until he closed his window.

"That better?"

"No." She rubbed her eyes and sniffed. Damn it, she might be crying or trying to trick him. He couldn't see her face, but heard the tremor in her voice.

She drew her feet up to sit on them. He turned on the heat. It was getting warm inside the truck. The beams from the headlights bounced on the road ahead almost hypnotic. The silence left a sleepy vacuum around them. She stirred, turning to face him. If she'd hit him in the face with a two-by four, he wouldn't have been more shocked by what she said next.

"I realize you're anxious to be rid of me, so I have a bargain to offer." She hesitated long enough for him to hear her shuddering intake of breath. "I'll do anything you want if you'll drive me to Denver and give me air fare to Puerto Vallarta."

The air exploded around him. If she's hit him in the face with a two-by four, he wouldn't have been more shocked. What had made her so scared she'd play the whore to escape? Why was she that afraid of the people in her past?

Until this moment, he'd not put his everything into taking care of her. She needed protection not only from a bungling, lowlife extremist, but her own son-of-a-bitch grandpa.

She had to be terrified to offer it up to him for the price of a ticket when she loathed him. The thought made him cringe.

He puffed on his cigar a final time before crushing it in the ashtray, and then lowered the window to toss out the dead stogie. Remembering how cold she'd been, he quickly closed the window.

She looked small and vulnerable in her corner of the seat. He huffed at his big, protective thoughts. Sacrifice and all that shit.

Who was he kidding? He'd bleed his last drop before handing her over to that man she called her grandfather. The old coot had a hell of a lot to answer for.

He drove the truck pell-mell along the winding road, glancing at her to find her pulling a shirt he'd dropped on the floor over her legs. It probably smelled like her now. He'd more than likely never wash it again just to keep her scent near him.

The ride seemed to be taking forever, and his legs cramped with tension. The lodge finally came into view through the line of young aspens he'd planted along the road. He took the corner fast, sliding to a stop in the driveway near the hitching post.

That was odd. These woman didn't know how to turn a light off, the place usually lit up like a circus, every light blazing until midnight. Right now, all the lights were off. That was a small miracle if not a sign of trouble.

He stopped her when she tried to open her door, taking her hand to ease her out on his side.

Damn. Something was going on at the lodge. Pulling Huffy down beside him, Turk took another wary look at the lights that were on in the stable and now in Huffy's window.

His heart bounced in his ribs and his breath chased after it. The bastard might be here, and no telling what had happened to Conner.

He raged inside, not knowing who his enemy was. That pimp Shane or Kufu Rama Fa looking for some hellfire?

The zigzag, swinging beam from a flashlight, strung razor wire around his nerves. Someone in the stable did a sloppy search. Well, they'd soon find something they didn't want.

He pushed her to the ground. "Stay here. Don't get up until I call you."

"Don't leave me!"

"Shh. I'll be back."

For a split second, the reflection off the side mirror blazed in her eyes. She was afraid whether she admitted it or not, and he had to leave her.

Pulling his Glock from the holster on the inside door panel, he crouched and moved toward the stable. He kept the moving light in sight, worried there may be more than one thug on his property.

His finger tightened against the trigger, and his legs tensed as a figure came running from the building.

He sucked in his breath, lowering his weapon.

Good God almighty. He'd almost shot Conner.

"Turk! You back?" Conner ran toward him, talking a mile a minute. "She's gone. I heard a door open upstairs and went to see what it was. The damned cat had opened her door and was messing around up there."

"Conner." Grabbing his arm, Turk tried to calm the excited young man. "She's with me."

"I swear she couldn't have slipped by me." Conner shook his head and slapped his hat on his thigh. "Ain't no way."

"Listen to me. She didn't slip by you, man. She left the house way before we put up our sentry."

"Slipped by you too, huh?" Conner struck a jaunty pose, hands on his hips. "I secured the other chicks in the hearth room. I think they'll be glad to get out of here in the morning."

"That doesn't surprise me." Turk walked back to the truck where Huffy crouched in the darkness. "Worst damn summer this place ever had."

He tossed a pebble at the truck fender, the rattle enough to scare her.

"Turk. Where are you?" Hearing her call his name was pleasant, and the thrill splintering through him unexpected.

"Right here." He leaned down, taking her hand. "Let's go to the house."

She still had that damn shirt in her fist. His gut clenched with an ache completely foreign, an intense, painful emotion.

He was being a fool now, softening up like a jerk that had never been off the farm. No use getting lace on his shorts over this woman. Huffy would leave here the moment this mess was cleared up.

That reminded him to make a few calls. He managed to get the pick up time scheduled with the bus company. That left one gnarly subject to settle. Sleeping arrangements were yet to be hammered out. *Damn.* His troubles only got worse at bedtime.

Conner walked them as far as the front porch, obviously anxious to be on his way. He looked back at his truck, and then took a couple backward steps. "If you want me to hang around until morning, I don't mind. If you can't handle things here."

Turk shook his head. "You have plans. Go ahead." He opened the door for Abigail, but thought to hold her back while talking with Conner. "I've made the call and placed the order for a couple of shuttles to pick up the ladies."

"Hasta la vista." Taking off his hat to sweep it in Abigail's direction, Conner took a few strides and hesitated, waiting to make sure all was well.

"My ass," Turk grumbled. He had eleven women waiting in the house, everyone capable of bashing his brains out. "I should make you go in first."

Conner trotted off toward his pickup the instant Turk gave him the wave to leave. "Call me." Mischievous laughter followed him from the darkness.

Turk pushed on the door and it swung open to reveal several faces peering from the darkened hearth room.

"Ladies. Come on out. Nothing to be scared of. It was just a coyote barking at the moon." He hung his hat on a peg near the front door, smiling at the group crowding around. "You can rest easy now. Get some shut-eye. We have an early start in the morning with those shuttle buses getting here at seven Am."

Sounds he equated to twittering birds and a sock hop broke the silence. His ladies were happy to be under his protection again. All except Huffy. She stood apart as the other women hugged him, finally filing by him to go upstairs.

He bolted the door, rattling off the reasons she was bunking with him.

Good God he was in trouble.

"Look, Huffy." He hesitated, looking into her eyes. "I'll move into the den section of my quarters. It's off the bedroom and I can hear anything that moves in the hall or stairs."

She licked her lips, and glanced at the door as if she would bolt for it. "About what I said earlier."

He waved off her explanation. "No need. You were upset."

"I was serious."

* * * *

Abigail didn't see it coming but felt the fracture of exploding anger and crystallized air splintering in the room around her. Turk clenched his jaw while he looked her up and down.

"Say what?"

His less than polite tone challenged her to repeat herself.

"I believe you understood me."

There was no reason to fear his action, no reason at all to fight when he grabbed her arm in his powerful hands, quickstepping her to the door of his room.

He bumped the door open with her weight, moving her inside his dimly lit sanctuary. The warm air was heavy with his scent, hugging her in its embrace, seeping into her clothing and skin.

He was everywhere, pressed to her, crowding her with his strong body, rousing a desire that threatened to suffocate her. His voice trickled from her earlobe down her spine to tingle in the center of her pulsing crotch.

"Want to clarify that, Ma'am?"

Abigail could see clearly she might die of passion if he touched her again, but she must stand up and maintain control. "No need to rehash it. I made my offer."

His fingers wove into her hair while his lips branded her neck with a trail of kisses so hot her lips parched. She wasn't certain of his words but knew they were dirty.

He spoke to her again, bucking against her to send a clearly defined idea of his powerful male parts. "What do you do best, baby?" His mouth closed over hers before she could peddle her wares, stopping her half-hearted little protests.

Liar, liar. She pretended to be unaffected by the touch of his firm lips working hers apart. She forced her body to stiffen while he sucked her lips in his mouth, her soft moan of surrender mewled in her throat.

He held her against the door, fondling her breasts. *Stop him!* A weak little voice whined from a cowardly hiding place. The heat from his hand enhanced the size of her breasts as he squeezed them in his fists, gently pressing the hard nipples until she gasped with pleasure.

He had more than her bra size on his mind. He pried her knees apart with his leg, and ripped her slacks open, his hand diving down inside to catch her pubic curls in his fingers. He growled against her ear.

"You want it standing up or on your back?"

Sensing insult in his voice, she caught his hand to hold his fingers away from her privates. "That's enough, you bastard!"

His fingers gripped her chin while he devoured her mouth with his, finally kissing her with such tender heat their lips fused together.

He let her go, as if they'd merely exchanged a word or two. "Next guy's not going to be as nice as me, Huffy."

The moment had passed for him, yet her heart continued to race. "I stand by what I said. I'll do anything to get away from you." She scrubbed her hand over her mouth. "You're a liar. There's no one trying to hurt me."

"Do whatever you want. Except leave."

She didn't scream or cry out in anger, or collapse in a heap of weeping femininity. If he had even the slightest inkling of the depth of her humiliation, he'd not hesitate to hurt her again.

Just one more man to scar your foolish heart.

Chapter 13

Abigail was afraid of the dark, and would never sleep with the windows open. She'd always been frightened of the dark. That had always been a bone of contention with her grandfather. He'd labeled her a coward and wasteful. Braving his wrath, she never turned off the tiny nightlight by her bed.

Still smarting from the combustive interlude with Turk, she pretended to be busy packing when several of the other guests poked their heads in the door to speak to her.

"You're coming back in December, aren't you Abigail?" Brenda's smile was a bit insincere. "I hear the sleigh rides and wiener roasts are to die for."

"I don't think so." Abigail couldn't believe what she was hearing. "You're not serious?"

"Quite." Brenda stroked her long red hair and closed her eyes. "I was here for the first winter, two years ago."

"Nice, huh?" Gritting her teeth with resentment, Abigail thought of Turk's ruthless way of treating her.

"Yes, lovely and so traditional. The Christmas tree touched the beams of the ceiling and Turk had bought gifts for all of the guests." Brenda sighed before making a more personal observation. "Its unfortunate Turk had to suffer such a horrible injury in the military."

"An injury?" Abigail's curiosity was on high. "What happened?"

"Oh, my yes." Brenda's excitement seemed to rise to the opportunity of sharing gossip. "Mind you, I don't know exactly what happened, but Dorene told Maude about it. She found out through a secret conversation with Glenda, the barmaid at Blue Bears Ball's."

Abigail's brows shot up. "Blue Ball's? You and the others socialize with the women there?"

"Well, not exactly." Brenda looked around as if making sure there was no one to snitch on her. "Maude goes there with Conner sometimes when he makes supply runs. She buys cartons of cigarettes."

"Brenda!" Bursting with curiosity, Abigail prompted the woman. "What did Glenda say about Turk's injury?"

"Well," Brenda's eyes narrowed and her voice slipped into a low murmur of conspiracy. "His wounds left him unable to, you know, do it."

"Are you sure she told the truth?"

"No, but he never touches any of us, poor dear." Brenda sighed. "What a waste." She covered her mouth and headed for the door. "That's not to be repeated."

"Of course not." Abigail closed her door and pondered Brenda's words.

She knew for a fact there was nothing wrong with Turk's sexual response. She'd known the heat and power of his arousal when he kissed her.

A sly smile skipped over her lips. This was something he'd cooked up with that dancehall floozy to keep the women at the lodge at bay.

Of all the egotistical, horses rears she'd known, Turk topped them all. She thought about the coming hours and possible days she might have to spend alone with him. A feeling of melancholy picked at her stomach.

Everyone would be gone tomorrow, everyone but her and the man with the war injury.

Whatever happened, happened. She remembered the wet bath towels draped over the rocker. She grabbed them and opened the closet door. The darn basket was overflowing and she didn't know how to operate the washer. The plain truth was, she knew nothing about running a home.

There really was no need. She had no desire to bend her back for any man and his demon seed. No way would she be caught in that net. You'd have to be insane to put up with a man's abuse for what passed as love.

A surge of cold expectation coursed through her. The position with the travel agency would more than make up for whatever she might lose out on here. She threw the towels in the basket, and tried to push the door shut. It popped open and she ignored it.

She sighed as she reclined on the bed. It was possible Turk would be too busy taking care of horses and cleaning to keep her under surveillance. Nodding with clear resolve, her plans burned in her mind. She would take the truck, and drive to Denver. Just before her plane departed, she'd call him and tell him where to find his truck.

The plan had some flaws. Of course she'd have to steal money from him as well. Getting to his wallet might not be so easy. Sex was probably the only way to pry it from his body. She closed her eyes while praying that her plans materialized.

Taking several books from a satchel, Abigail curled up against the stack of pillows to read. Sonnets written in the romance languages of French and Spanish were like paintings to her, rich and beautiful to the heart.

Reaching under the pillows, she brought out a plump, fruit-filled Hermit cookie. The heavenly aroma made her mouth water.

She started to take a bite, but hesitated, thinking she might need this morsel tomorrow. After all, Cookie would not be there and she didn't know the business end of a stove. She carefully wrapped the morsel in a tissue and slipped it back under the pillows.

Going back to reading was impossible. She'd made the mistake of letting herself think about tomorrow. The hollow ache in her stomach had nothing to do with hunger and everything to do with fear.

She couldn't believe there was nothing more than this to life. No, damn it. She had a purpose, a future if only Shane would help her. This time of evening, those big ugly bugs set off in a steady, sawing buzz. He'd called them locusts when she'd screamed in terror after one lit on her back.

Tears came for no good reason, except she'd never been so lonely. They splashed onto the fine linen pages of her book. Weeping was for other women, the ones with something to lose. At that moment, Abigail couldn't think of a single reason for her tears.

Like every other night at the lodge, she slipped off the bed and opened her door a sliver, bracing it open with her house slipper. No one had ever mentioned the shoe in the door, but certainly they had all seen it. For all she knew, they did the same thing.

She hurried back to bed, looking around the room before turning off the bedside lamp. She pulled the sheet and quilt up under her chin, glancing at the ray of soft light coming from the hall light.

Tonight she would be all right.

* * * *

Turk didn't need an alarm clock. His body was attuned to waking at dawn and his feet hit the floor at first light. This was going to be a hectic morning with all the women leaving Lone Horse.

He was ready for the frantic running back and forth, the last minute search for one thing or another forgotten, misplaced item.

He didn't want to dwell on what would happen later. It made him nervous.

He went into the shower, eyes half closed and a need for coffee prodding him forward. The noticeable absence of the delectable aroma reminded him the job of making coffee and cooking fell to him today.

There wasn't time to linger under the shower spray this morning. The shuttle buses would be here long before the women were ready.

Somehow his decision to make the lodge a hideout for chicks seemed a little crazy this early in the day.

The cool morning air was abruptly split by someone's boom box winding down a rousing session with Hank Williams Jr. That was his cue to kick it into high gear and get dressed. The women were going to need him.

In his haste, he nicked his face in several places while wielding the razor, pulled on a pair of socks with holes in them, and a shirt missing several buttons. His worn jeans had a hole deep in the pocket.

He left his quarters and headed for the kitchen. Time to pull KP. While the big pot of java perked, he nuked several dozen breakfast sandwiches, cut up fruit and laid out plates, and cups along with eating utensils.

"Perfect."

His droll comment complimented his mood.

Satisfied with his handiwork, Turk went out to the hallway and was quickly converged upon by a horde of laughing, playful women.

Turk couldn't hold back his laughter as the group hugged him, Brenda daring to plant a kiss on his mouth.

"Hey, now, ladies." He directed the crowd to the kitchen. "Better chow down. It'll be a long ride to Denver. Breakfast is ready."

His thoughts went to one beautiful woman with soft, plump lips that tasted of cherry. She'd probably say she wasn't, but Huffy would be hungry.

He exhaled with dread. She'd come down when she was angry enough.

Meanwhile, he'd have time to take care of the horses and feed the blamed cat. Maybe Huffy would want to go for a swim before it got too late in the day. Fat chance. She didn't want to do anything with him but put buckshot in his ass.

Twittering noises brought his thoughts back to the packed kitchen. The ladies were polishing off the sandwiches when the shuttles arrived, honking their horns.

Gleeful pandemonium broke out. Turk was being hugged and kissed and even saw a few tears as his guests left the lodge for the season. They piled in the shuttle busses and waved from the windows, blowing kisses and yelling his name.

Turk stood in the driveway, watching the overloaded vans drive out of sight. It was all over but the war. Speaking of war, he looked up at Huffy's window in time to see her peering down at him.

"Morning, Huffy." He smiled at her before thinking. "Get dressed and have a bite to eat. We're going to the stable."

The curtains flipped down. He shrugged, convinced he'd have a rough day with the last remaining guest. Damn, why did she have to be so contrary?

He'd barely made it into the house before she called down her answer. "I'm not going, you know."

"Yeah, you are."

After that, the silence was deafening from the entry hall all the way to the kitchen. But that's what he liked. Like hell.

Walking out to the hall, he grimaced after touching the gaping material where a button should have been. If he got the time, he'd bundle up all his duds that needed fixing and take them to Glenda.

Right now, he had to figure out a way to keep the peace with Huffy.

At the foot of the stairs, he began his quest in the taming of his wild Arizona rose.

Chapter 14

Abigail heard a new tone to his voice. Consideration?

She'd watched as the other's left and the way Turk had stood out in the driveway until they were gone.

So that's why he'd called her. He wanted company. And a farm hand to help with the animals.

"Abigail." She jumped when he shouted her name. He meant business. "I don't give a rats ass if you're in the mood or not, but the horses are not going hungry because you're in a snit. Now, get your ass down here."

Her lungs seemed to have collapsed from the shock of his words. After what had happened in his darkened room, she knew he didn't make idol threats.

Hurry you fool. He'd love to see you naked.

A familiar shiver licked its way over her breasts.

She scowled, hating herself for finding the idea exciting. He was probably brutal during lovemaking. She shivered with apprehension.

Remembering the way he'd touched and kissed that woman at Blue Bears Ball's, hot disgust at her sexual yearnings for the man shot through her.

Expecting to hear his boots on the stairs any second, Abigail raced around the cluttered room, dressing with no sense of fashion that morning.

Feverishly pulling items from hangers, she yanked on her outfit.

The small amount of self-assurance she possessed drained away as she stared at the diaphanous and brazen looking lounge outfit she wore. Bright red!

The sheer tomato colored lounge pants would be nothing but a tease to the heathen downstairs. She had given no thought to her undergarments before dragging the outfit onto her body. No bra and the tiniest panties she owned would be perfect.

She had to be out of her mind. No. She was out of time. He was a savage and probably preferred bare feet.

Knowing the rough ground out by the barn, she grabbed up the soft black slippers that caught her eye and slipped them on.

A tingle of nervous energy zipped along her spine as she pinned her hair up in a loose knot, and secured it with fancy Japanese picks.

Catching the reflection of her outfit in the small mirror, she had a moment of doubt. The top was nothing more than a see through pin-tucked camisole. Seeing so much breast and nipple startled her.

Nonsense, coward. He'll love it.

Taking a deep breath, she hurried to the stair landing, somewhat afraid but determined. It made no difference. What ever he did, she had no choice but to go along with it.

He waited at the foot of the steps, gazing at her with a no nonsense stare. "Turk?" He didn't speak until she stood in front of him.

"What do you say, we don't talk?" His gaze didn't flicker away, only clung more tightly to her body. "Let's go."

"What do you want me to do?" He gazed at her, and something wild simmered in his gaze.

"Be quiet, stay close and don't give me any trouble." He touched her shoulder. "I don't have time to waste while you pick out the proper shoes for the day."

"I don't want to keep the horses waiting. Lead the way."

Her smart aleck choice of wearing shoes with no real sole made her regret the show of independence. Gravel cut into the flimsy material and her contrived, saucy walk became nothing more than a hobbling limp of pain.

"I told you to get your shoes." Had that been a smirk in his voice? He pointed to the edge of the path. "Stay on the grass."

"You expect me to walk the rest of the way?" She sucked her breath in for emphasis. "It's a long way to the stable."

"You expect me to carry you?" With his usual maddening show of intolerance, Turk stopped in mid-stride. "You made your choice. Same as always. Live with it."

She swiped at her dilapidated hairdo that fell around her face. "You can't possibly know how much I hate you. You're a disgusting barnyard animal, not fit to touch me."

"If I wanted to touch you, I wouldn't ask." He grinned at her, gesturing to her drooping pants. "You'll have to clean up first."

His comment stung, but damn if she'd let him know.

He seemed to have forgotten her, getting several steps ahead. She leaned down to scoop up a handful of gravel, and flung it at his broad shoulders.

Abigail wasn't sure what she expected. He didn't react, only reset his damn Stetson and walked on. She figured that could mean trouble later, or perhaps he had no feeling in his hide.

A pleasant diversion came in the form of a patch of newly bloomed wild flowers near the barn. She took time to gather a handful, sniffing them until she looked up to see Turk glaring at her.

"Are you through?" He inclined his head to the open doors of the stable. "Grab a shovel."

The first thing she noticed inside the warm stable was the smell of horses along with the aroma of sweet mash and grain. It wasn't offensive at all, but she refused to let him know she didn't mind being there.

She shrank back when he handed her two halters. "Am I to wear these?"

"Probably be too small." Turk wrapped the reins around her wrist. "Get Maude and Tilly out and walk them to the corral. I'll run the rest of the herd out."

Okay, she could deal with the two docile mares. Getting the halters on them was a snap. The two mares nuzzled her arm for treats they always expected.

"Stop it. I don't have anything for you. I haven't even had breakfast yet. Probably won't get any."

Snapping a shank onto the halters, she led them a few steps before they morphed into frightening creatures.

They became unruly, nudging her with their big heads as she walked between them. The corral gate was open and she tried to lead them toward it. Her heart jumped into her throat as her feet left the ground. The mares were in competition for treats and began nipping at each other over Abigail's head, lifting her off the ground.

She'd never noticed before the mare's enormous yellow teeth that popped viciously together near her face. Hauled up to stare into their wild, rolling eyes, she thought she might be heading for death. Kicking her feet did nothing to separate them, not even her screams of terror.

Turk had had heard her cries of desperation and ran to separate the battling horses.

She had never been so glad to see another human being. He grabbed the bridles of both horses, forcing them apart.

She grabbed him around the neck, holding on to him for dear life.

"Huffy. I told you to walk them, not tease 'em."

He ruined the moment and squashed her gratitude.

"I didn't need you."

He pushed her aside. "Go muck out a stall."

Turk controlled the mares with little more than his touch while the rest of the herd trotted out to browse on the fresh alfalfa scattered around the corral.

She didn't want any trouble, clamping her mouth shut as she picked her way over the rocks to the stable.

Inside, she found her a shovel and a pair of scuffed, dried out leather boots. They were five sizes too big and tripped her on every other step, but she didn't care. The legs of her pants dropped into the boot tops.

She set to work, scooping up horse dung and throwing it into a wheelbarrow. He joined her, working in the next stall. The warm air filled with dust and loose straw, making her sneeze and clung to her tangled hair.

She followed him down the row of stalls, cleaning the ones he left for her. Some of them were clean and she pretended to be mucking as he'd said.

Taking a five second break, she caught him eyeing her over a stall, his grin sexy, and almost making her forget how much she despised him. He shook his head and went back to work.

He taught her how to mix the oats and mash, holding her hand as she dipped it from the big sacks and into buckets. As he leaned over to help her, she wanted to wriggle with anticipation just looking at the olive gold skin at his open collar.

While she wiped sweat from her face, he handed her a can of saddle dressing. Speechless, she glared into his eyes, forcing him to explain.

"For the saddle you straddled all summer."

"My saddle asked for dressing?"

"Just get busy working it into the seat." He scooped a generous amount out on his fingers, wiping it into her palm. "Nice smooth strokes. Don't hurt it."

She grimaced, dabbing a tiny bit on the tooled seat of her saddle. At least it didn't smell to high heaven. He watched her with a glower, his scrubbing gestures suggesting she wasn't using enough soap or effort.

Bone tired, she took a break, drinking several cups of cold water from the cooler. She was shocked to see it was eleven-thirty. He'd been working her all morning and she was famished.

He could read her mind obviously, tossing a glove to get her attention. "Let's break for lunch."

"If you must." No reason to make him think she was weakening. His eyes twinkled, and his quick grin spoke clearly of his amusement at her bravado.

He let her go outside first, turning off the lights in the stable. Tripping like a clown in her enormous boots, Abigail followed him up the trail to the back door.

"Leave those boots outside, Huffy."

"I didn't mind wearing them."

"I don't want field mice in here."

Fear and revulsion took over, her bottom lip curling with disgust as she removed the boots and flung them out the door.

"You could have told me those were nasty." The thought of squishing a mouse with her bare foot sent a shiver over her. "When do I get food?"

He dropped the bag of English muffins he held, pointing to his office. "After you see what I've been putting up with."

Her face screwed up in a look of disgust, but she followed him.

"Sit." Turk took a large stack of papers from a drawer, dropping them on the desk. "I'm probably making a mistake, but read. Its about time you knew how much crap you're in and how much trouble you're causing me."

He was serious and she was frightened. "Take me to the airport. Do that, and I won't be any more trouble. Please."

"So that's how it's going to be." He pushed her back down in the chair when she tried to get up. "It's not that simple, Huffy. Aren't you interested in how the reports describe you and Shane the boy wonder?"

"I really hate your attitude."

"That's okay."

She eyed him with suspicion. He held the big, old fashioned, leather office chair until she settled in it. "This is crazy. I haven't done anything wrong."

"You just pick the wrong men, Huffy." He placed a thick stack of papers in front of her.

Abigail breathed over the knot of fear in her throat. Curiosity made her begin to read.

She reread the first several paragraphs. Yes, there was her name and Shane's as well. Personal information only she should know.

Seeing her self described as a willful runaway and frequent troublemaker, a woman of loose morals and perhaps mentally challenged. Anyone reading this would have to think she was a whore. All this from her grandfather. She refused to cave in to emotion, but found it difficult to control the tremble of her hands.

She was furious, crushed by the humiliation of the typed words swimming before her eyes. How could he paint her in such vulgar terms and in an open and public way? She'd supposedly brought shame to the fine name of Van Huffington.

Now, there were horrid things about Shane. The guy that she loved like a brother accused of being connected to a terrorist group. It was too ridiculous to believe.

She couldn't believe her own grandfather had given out such private information, most of it nothing but lies.

Turk returned, quietly placing a cup on the desk near her. "Are you ready to tell me what's going on?"

She swiped the papers off the desk and got to her feet. "This is all garbage?"

"Tell me something I can believe, Huffy."

"You've already made up your mind." She paced the floor, kicking the papers aside. "I know one thing. No man can be trusted."

"Not true."

"Then take me to the airport. I can get to my grandmothers and out of this country."

"What's so damned important somewhere else?"

"My life, that's all!"

"What the hell does that mean?" His words were tinged with irritation.

"As hard as it is for you to believe, I have a position. Or, as hillbillies call them, a job. A real job with a travel agency in Britain." She visualized her life, fast flowing down the drain to dismal failure. "I'm not a beggar that lives off other people. I earned my degrees and found employment on my own." Her traitorous voice broke. "It makes no difference now. I've lost everything."

"The old man must have some reason to worry about your lifestyle."

There was no mistake, his low simmering desire for her was edged with jealousy over a man she'd never slept with.

"You want to ask about all the men in the report."

He glanced away, then his gaze settled on her face. "I won't lie. I'm curious."

"They were all decent to me. I may have been in love with several of them."

Turk showed no emotion other than the slightest narrowing of his eyes. "So, why all the running? Stand up for yourself."

Typical male. He'd never been afraid of anything or anyone. Big, strong, bully, never taking any guff off another person. She wanted to inflict pain on him. Instead, she remained calm.

"I can't stay." A tremor from deep inside her persisted to nag, the desire to lean on him, to let him shield her from fear and trouble. She shook off the feeling. That wasn't real life. There was only herself to rely on. "I can't let my grandfather find me. He's found a man that's willing to overlook my wild ways. I won't go back!"

Turk cursed under his breath. "Trust me, even if it's just for tonight. Abigail."

"But you don't know what my grandfather can make happen."

Turk snorted with obvious amusement. "He doesn't know what a Gunnison can make happen."

She didn't question him, simply accepted the fact that the life she'd worked for had evaporated and she'd use Turk until circumstances changed. "I'm sure."

"That's it?" He leaned against the door jam, apparently waiting for something apologetic from her.

She nodded. "You mentioned lunch. Will I still be fed rations?"

His sultry gaze was answer enough. "We'll work something out."

* * * *

What was she thinking now? That blue gaze hovered over him like an approaching storm.

Get hold of your self, man. Huffy's just trying out her baby teeth on you.

Turk read people well enough to know she'd been hurt by the report. He couldn't understand a family that felt nothing but fear and anger towards each other.

And here she was, in his kitchen, soft and sweet looking, even with hay in her hair and dirt on her beautiful face.

He flushed with disgusting inadequacy under her steady gaze. Somehow, he felt like a mouse being watched by a tiger.

What a jerk he'd become, thinking in terms better suited to one of those chick flicks.

He flipped eggs onto a plate along with a toasted muffin. With the aplomb of a wild boar, he dug out jelly from a canning jar for her pleasure.

"Sit."

"I'd rather stand."

Of course she chose to stand. *Damn it.*

Where had the ornery minx gone, and when did the mind blowing temptress takeover? A short time ago, she was throwing rocks at him, now he could smell female honey.

She took long, agonizing minutes to lick the wild strawberry jam from the muffin. Her lips became red with the sweet jelly. He shook in his boots just hearing her soft moan of pleasure.

"You don't wear many clothes, do you?"

He had spoken aloud when his feelings became too intense. It had been an observation more than a question.

"Does that turn you on Cowboy?" She lifted her small, barefoot, planting it on the chair, looking like a seductive peasant.

"Like a butane torch."

Caught in a trap of his own making, Turk moved dangerously near her, the scent of Persian Lilac reached for him with invisible silken arms, but he felt it in every red corpuscle in his body.

His gaze licked over her, tasting her closeness like a starving animal. His raging imagination allowed him to free her rosy nipples to his lips, the sweetness of the firm buds almost flooring him. "You have jelly on your breast."

"Oh, my." She let her head fall back, exposing her throat and the pulse that throbbed under her smooth skin. "Show me."

His arms went around her, claiming her completely. She was in his blood, dragging him into that burning crazy ring of fire. He'd lost his mind, not caring about rules or regulations, not Gun, and not the other men she'd known.

Consumed with burning need to take Huffy destroyed his common sense, leaving Turk with only blinding desire. No way to get out, hell he didn't want out, he wanted sex with Huffy.

All he could hear and make sense of was that damn sensation of free falling—down, down, down…in a raging fire. Oh, hell yes, he'd wanted to go down, to give his wild Arizona rose the deep pleasure of her life.

The flames licked around him. She'd been caught up in that same heat, wrapping her arms around his neck, pulling his face to hers to slip her sweet tongue into his eager mouth. Oh yeah, the fire was out of control.

"You drive me crazy, Huffy." He held her face in his hands to cover her lips in a hard, deep kiss, soft lips that parted for his tongue.

Like the finest satin, best cognac, that's what she felt and tasted like. He experienced a kind of passion that most likely would kill him before it ended.

The taste of sweet told him to never let it end and he pulled back to lick the jam from the mounds of her creamy breast. She gasped, clutching at his shoulders, her eyes dark and filled with a hungry glow. He still held that damned jelly container, a little of the contents dribbled onto her throat. The taste of her was just as he'd fantasized, the opulence of her body so much sexier.

Her soft intakes of breath became the feminine moans of a woman on fire. Damn formality. He licked and sucked his way over her lovely flesh, pulling the camisole up to free the fine creamy mounds of her breasts, greed taking over as he pulled each nipple into his mouth. He knew she was hot for him now, her hands tearing at his shirt and the buttons of his jeans.

Sweet, hard and hot, and the flames leaped higher. He was burning with desire to feel everything about her, the firm, smooth skin of her back and stomach, the warm press of her tits to his chest. And it burned, red hot in their circle of fire.

He tried to speak, but nothing happened for a breathless second. "I want you, baby, right here, right now." His voice rasped with passion.

"Stop making me wait, Cowboy." No holding back for her, the way she wrapped her leg around his waist and ground her hips to his took him closer to divine pleasure.

"I'm so all over you, Miss Abigail." With one sweep of his hand, dishes, jelly jars and muffins were cleared from the table.

Their hands worked as a team, yanking her pants down, unbuttoning his fly.

Turk wasn't bothered that he couldn't breathe, that his heart pounded in his ears and his blood had probably become ashes.

They went on a mad, wonderful tumbling flight together, arms and legs tangling into a love knot. She arched to him, taking his throbbing erection in her hand, guiding him to her warm center where his tip brushed the entrance to bliss.

He shook like an aspen in the winter wind, hands clumsy and his heart afraid.

My God, Gunnison, you've waited for so long.

No more waiting, no more painful disappointment. He drove into her, losing all sense of being earthbound, his blood rushing like liquid steel through his veins.

Hearing her cries of enjoyment spurred him on, his single thought to hear her say his name when she came. She was tight and well equipped to take all of him, her fine ass holding his weight with no trouble. He wanted to see all of her, but couldn't pull from the garden of pleasure she had let him enter.

Turk didn't mind the biting furrows her nails made in his back when her climax came, her sobbing cry of "Turk, hold me Turk." He'd given her good sex and now he could let go in a life threatening orgasm.

Coming with Huffy was world shattering different for him. Painful was his first thought until his head almost spun off his shoulders. He grabbed for her, holding on until the ecstasy had passed and pure exhaustion slammed into him.

He was wrung dry, left with nothing but the strength to kiss her and moan in a strange wonderful pain.

"Huffy, why did you make me wait so long?" He lifted his head to look in her eyes, warmed by the soft look of satisfaction he saw there. "You took me there, baby. Took me there."

"Let's get another jar of jelly." She stroked his ass with a gentleness that belied the plow marks in his back.

Ping.

He knew that sound.

Small arms fire, maybe.

No, too little, no explosion.

Ping. Ping.

He lifted her from the table, waiting until she gripped his waist with her legs. She seemed to know something was wrong, probably sensed his concern.

He'd forgotten a very important rule. The war wasn't over.

There it was again, only more insistent now. Sounded like pebbles hitting the windowpanes. The sound of rocks smacking into the glass confirmed his suspicions. Trouble had come calling.

"We have a problem, Huffy." He let her down, quickly buttoning his jeans and shrugging on the shreds of his shirt. "Fix your clothes."

He couldn't help the impatience in his gut as she messed with her pants and top. Like a frightened quail, she darted for the bathroom and ran water. He wanted to yell at her to hustle it up like he would have a raw recruit, but held his tongue. Looking a little pale under her sex flush, she hurried back to stand beside him. She looked up at him with worry in her eyes.

"I'm dressed."

"You're fine." He took her hand, leading her to the back door. She fussed with her ripped camisole. "Stop worrying. You're covered."

Yeah, sure she was. Those see through pants and no panties were a laugh, except this wasn't funny.

More pebbles hit the glass of the entry hall. That was enough. He made his choice and led her to the kitchen, not knowing how many guns were outside.

He opened the back door, stepping out cautiously to make sure the coast was clear. With Huffy close behind, he moved toward the front of the house, hoping to take the thugs by surprise.

He stopped and whispered to her. "The keys are in the truck. If I go down, head for Blue Bears." He kept her behind him as he cornered the house, drawing down on the person causing trouble on his property.

"Freeze, son-of-a-bitch."

Chapter 15

Abigail screamed in terror when she recognized the intruder. "Shane!"

She tore free of the iron grip on her arm, and raced to where the wide-eyed young man stood. Without thinking, she threw herself against him, falling to the ground in a protective action.

From behind her she heard Turk's curse of exasperation and stared in fright at his jean clad legs as she hovered over Shane.

"Are you crazy?" He was furious and continued to yell at her first, then poor Shane. "I take it your the son-of-a.... That guy from Canada."

Abigail pushed Turk's hand away, still afraid he intended to use that huge gun on the helpless guy she held down.

"He's not dangerous. Shane does not use guns."

"Aw, hell." Turk shoved the weapon in his waistband. "Get up. Come in the house. I don't know who might be following you."

The pounding of her heart calmed as relief set in. "Shane, why didn't you call and let me know you were here?"

"On what?" He laughed, like always in the face of adversity. "I lost my cell phone and don't have a dime."

Sympathy for him softened her voice. "How did you get here?"

"My car gave out way back on the highway. Walked the rest of the way."

The abrupt way he stopped smiling meant Turk was glaring at him. He still had heartbreaker good looks and black curling hair that needed a trim. Most noticeable was the pansy blue of his heavily lashed eyes. Instead of the Hollywood idol he could have been, Shane was broke and in trouble.

She took her nervous friends arm. "You're probably hungry." His limping gait concerned her.

He nodded, glancing warily at Turk. "Yeah, I could stand a bite. Haven't eaten in several days."

"I'll feed you, and you're going to spill your guts while you eat." Turk patted the vicious guns handgrip. "Understand?"

Turk's breaking into their conversation didn't surprise her. He kept his hand on that gun as they walked to the kitchen door, looking around like a wolf on the hunt.

"Yeah." Shane nodded, holding on to her a little tighter.

Abigail felt sorry for her friend, his cheeks were lean and his body felt small against her. She caught Turk's look of speculation as she helped the unexpected company to a chair.

"You can go do whatever you were going to do, Turk. I'll feed him."

How could she have been so foolish? Of course he wouldn't leave. He already hated the youthful man at his table. Now he wanted to question him like some Gestapo agent.

"You talk, I'll fix his grub." He touched her hair. "You're probably still hungry too."

His small show of affection pleased her more than any gift she'd ever received. He smiled at her from across the room while he fixed more eggs and biscuits.

The message in his gaze reminded her of their passion only a short time ago. She ached to resume that delicious game.

Her thoughts probably showed on her face. Shane eyed her with a grin when she looked away from Turk.

"Did I get here too soon or too late?" He bit off a hunk of the ripe pear he'd taken from the fruit bowl.

Turk shook his head and stirred the Bisquick mix. Abigail flushed to her roots after looking down at her torn, jelly stained, transparent camisole.

She brushed at the dust on his sleeve. "Never mind that." He appeared so thin and beaten, her heart cried for him. Sliding a plea for understanding at Turk, she touched the huge blue knot on his hand. "Who did this to you? My family had you beaten?"

The sound of the oven door slamming started Abigail as well as Shane. Turk grabbed three mugs from the dish cupboard, and brought them to the table along with the coffee pot.

His dark visage spoke volumes of his mood, his hand clamped on the coffee pot like iron claws as he filled the mugs. Distrustful of Shane, protective of her, and anger all rolled into one seething rage.

He sat across from her and quirked an eyebrow. "Go ahead, malcontent, tell her what you've been up to. She'll be proud."

Shane tossed the remnants of the pear on the table, wiped his mouth and grinned. "Getting the hell beat out of me, that's what."

She wanted to cry, but the glower on Turk's face warned her to stifle her emotions. She got up, no longer concerned about her dress and hugged Shane's neck. "I'll take him to my room. I'm paid up for another week, am I not?"

Turk hesitated for a split second before confirming her statement. "Yeah, that's right."

"He needs rest and food." She attempted to help Shane from the chair, and draped his arm over her shoulders, glancing back at Turk. "He won't be able to work while he's here. I'll do his chores."

Okay, she'd said something that incensed the Lord and master of Lone Horse Lodge, the message conveyed by Turk's grimace and his hands lifting toward the ceiling.

"I have an idea." He put his leg out in front of her. "You go on upstairs and fix a room for him. Old Shane and I have to talk."

Abigail stepped over his long leg and sweat over the decision she had to make. This meant a serious browbeating for Shane, but he could take it.

"All right." She held her camisole together and patted Shane's back. "I'll do that and come back for you."

Turk laid a restraining hand on their guest's arm. "No need you coming back down. I'll help him upstairs if he needs it."

In her heart, she knew Turk wouldn't physically harm Shane, but he could tear him apart with his abrupt method of questioning.

Taking several steps, she paused. "I'll expect him shortly."

Turk's gaze should have frozen her to the floor, but he looked away before that happened, inclining his head toward the staircase. "Trust me. I'll send him up to you in one piece."

The ice in his voice left no doubt he resented the presence of this stranger in his house.

At the moment, the object of his annoyance was stuffing leftover breakfast croissants in his mouth. She hurried out of the room and up the steps before she broke into tears.

Maybe she should listen at the door to what was said in the kitchen. That wouldn't be wise. There was no way to be sneaky enough to outwit Turk.

Turk waited until Huffy had gone before firing his first question at Shane. "So, what's your story?"

The guy sat slouched in his chair, his hair uncombed and his beard several days old. Turk knew that most females panted after this grungy waif look.

He prowled behind Shane's chair, observing the young man's body language. When he answered, he did it with forthright disarming honesty.

"My story? Man, just one big mistake."

"I'll be the judge of that. And, don't call me *man*."

"Yes, sir."

Turk grimaced. "You're smart enough to know what I want to hear."

"I just came here to get Abbey. Not start trouble."

"Much to late for that, pal." Turk sat on the tables edge, gaze burning into Shane's tired looking eyes. "Who, what, and damn you, why?"

After a deep sigh, Shane opened up. "Abbey and I met in Dallas two years a go." He grinned as if he had a secret, then quickly lowered his chin. "She was in a bad relationship and staying away from her crazy grandfather as much as possible."

"The hockey player?" Turk's question was immediately followed by another. "What about her crazy grandfather?"

"Oh, man. Er, you don't want to know about that."

"Don't tell me what I want to know." Turk leaned across the table to glare at Shane. "What's the story there, then we'll move on to you."

"Mister Huffington put money in a checking account for her. She likes expensive clothes and partied hard. Spent the dough as soon as he deposited it."

Turk scowled. "Hell, that's not new. No reason for her to be running from him."

Shane looked longingly at the coconut cake in its glass-domed cover. "Is that okay to eat?"

"Have all you want, but hurry it up. I want to know the rest of the story."

Cutting a man-sized slice, Sane held it in his hand and ate as he talked. "She called me one day and asked if I had any spare money. Naturally I didn't. She broke down and cried, something I'd never heard her do."

Turk began to feel like a first class intruder in their lives. "What happened? Was she sick, or afraid?"

"Naw, she'd spent all of her month's allowance and wanted to go to her grandmother's."

That damned cake was uppermost on the kid's mind and it infuriated Turk. Then, he remembered how hungry he'd been out in the desert and jungle. "I gather she had a damned good reason to want to make the trip."

"Mister Van Huffington treated her like one of his stock options or something. He owned her and her future. Bought her anything she wanted, but made sure she was never over loaded with cash. Just a debit card good only in Phoenix."

Turk rubbed his jaw and thought over the description of Huffy's grandfather. "She doesn't look deprived to me. Who paid for this place?"

"I did."

"Why not get her plane tickets?"

"I ran out of money. That's why I hooked up with the Arab. I needed funds quick."

A reluctant grain of understanding rubbed Turk's sense of compassion. "Okay. Tell me about the Kufu Rama Fa and what went down."

Shane licked his lips and swallowed the last of his cake. "He approached me in a singles bar after Abbey left for the evening. He said he needed a courier with smarts. Of course I jumped on that. The money was phenomenal plus all expenses."

"Did you tell anyone about the job? Huffy, maybe?"

"No. She'd been crying that night over her asshole boyfriend. Plus, she'd just gotten word her application had been accepted for the job in the UK. I called her later that night to tell her about her reservation here. "

"So, why was she still crying?"

"Afraid to make a move. The old man, or her grandfather I mean, had found some rich dude to take her off his hands. An Earl or Lord of something."

"Women don't have to do that anymore."

"He could make it happen."

He'd never asked this of any other man about any other woman, but Turk was crumbling with curiosity. "Were you and Huffy more than friends?"

"Sure. She loves me and I'm crazy for her."

He didn't know which had hurt the most, a bullet in his back or Shane's loving admission. *Damn.*

"Okay. Back to Kufu. Did you know what you'd be carrying?"

"No idea. Just knew I was supposed to meet him in Los Alamos and take charge of a briefcase. I thought it might be hot diamonds or something like that. When I got there, I expected we might be going to a protest rally against the establishment or some kind of fun protest. Not just a damn briefcase and a ticket to Yemen." His smooth forehead creased in a frown. "If it had been two tickets to the UK, we'd have been okay ."

Turk sipped his cold coffee, grimacing at the bitter taste. That was only part of the reason for his frown.

"You can't be serious, fella? This day in age? Middle Eastern guy, Los Alamos, briefcase full of Lord knows what. Big money to play delivery boy."

"I needed money, and lots of it. For Abbey. She had plans."

"And he finally told you what was in the case?"

"Yeah. When I said I'd changed my mind, he tried to shoot me. I hit him with the case and got away, but not before he threatened to kill me and everyone I knew. I threw the case in some weeds near the building. I wasn't worried about my parents. They live in Canada."

Turk closed his eyes, trying to visualize what had occurred on that dark night. If not for the dire situation, it probably would have been good for a laugh.

"I want to know how Huffy fits in here, and what the Arab has planned for her."

"Oh, she doesn't figure in here at all."

Shane's ignorance about the ways of the world fanned the embers of anger for Turk. "How does this sound to you? That son-of-a-bitch isn't going to let you live, and he isn't known to leave witnesses to anything he's done. Get the picture?"

"Yeah. He's going to kill me."

Turk pointed to the ceiling. "And?"

"You don't think...not Abbey?" His big blue eyes got bigger, then shuttered in what Turk figured was remorse. "Abbey has nothing to do with this. I'll leave and she won't be in danger."

"You should have been thinking like this weeks ago." Handing the scared looking kid an apple, Turk exhaled wearily. "You leaving won't change a damn thing. No use you buying the farm somewhere on the highway. We'll work something out."

Shane's face crumpled with worry, yet he gnawed the apple like a starved bear cub. "I can't thank you enough, Mister Gunnison."

He didn't want to like Shane, wanted to belittle him, but Turk couldn't manage to browbeat the guy. His mind was on the sweet woman upstairs and she needed him even if she didn't know it.

Chapter 16

She'd clenched her teeth and went up to her room, wanting desperately to know what was going on in that kitchen. For the first time, she realized what a disgraceful mess she presented to the world with telltale bite marks on her throat, and a cherry colored whisker burn on her chin. Now she wanted to cry. Straw fell from her tangled hair and dirt hid under her nails. Turk probably had used her with revulsion and desperation.

Stop pitying yourself. You had a marvelous time on that table. So did he.

Tearing off the soiled clothing, she ran into the bathroom to step in the shower, letting the cold water punish her a little before the hot kicked in.

Half a bottle of shampoo and body wash later, she turned off the water and quickly dried herself. Her moisture lotion released the scent of lilacs as it warmed on her skin.

She pulled on a comfortable pink terry robe and tied it securely about her waist. Straightening the room took a few minutes, finding a place to put everything was a challenge. The crumpled papers on the bed were scooped in to the wastebasket, and curling irons, bottles and brushes were swept into the dressing table drawer. Her dirty clothing was tossed in the closet and the door shut securely.

The door opened and Shane eased in the room, looking around before speaking. "Damn, Abbey. We sure picked a hell of a place to get marooned."

She was in his arms then, hugging him close and patting his back.

"What happened Shane?" He held her tight, exhaling softly as she questioned him. "Are you mixed up with a terrorist?"

"I didn't know what they were until I got to Los Alamos. I found out they were stealing classified material and I was supposed to take it on to France."

"Are you crazy? What did you think you were carrying?"

"I thought maybe diamonds or some new medicine."

"Shane! You can't keep doing these things."

His sense of daring do kicked in. "I thought we were going to hold a week long anti-Government rally. You know, signs, bull horns." He gave her his stunning grin. "Kufu told me we were going to send a message to the fat cats in Washington. There were lots of the same people I'd picketed with a week before at a fur company."

"Just like college."

He shrugged. "Yeah. Just like college."

"You have to stop thinking like that." She closed the door. "Those men are looking for you, and know you are meeting me here."

His expression changed from playful to somber. "I'll leave tonight."

"No. They plan on killing both of us."

His breath whispered from his lips. "Why you? You have nothing to do with this."

She pressed her hand to his mouth. "We're friends. They don't know how much I am involved and don't care." His deep scowl and questioning gaze made her charge ahead. "Turk showed me every line of information the Government has on us, and those killers. We have to stay here until this man, Kufu is taken into custody."

"I'm so sorry, my Abbey. So sorry." He looked out the window. "I don't know how to set things straight. I have put you in terrible danger and that guy downstairs would love to put a slug in my heart."

His impression of Turk shocked her. "That's not true. He's worried about both of us."

"You two got a thing going on?" He flicked at the ruffle on the crisp curtain. "It shows when you look at each other."

"It's just a thing, Shane."

"Looked pretty serious to me. I thought you'd found the right one this time."

The emotions she'd so carefully quieted fought to escape her trembling heart. "I think he is the right one, Shane, but he isn't ready to fall in love."

"He's a mush brain if he lets you go."

She turned the bed down and patted the pillows. "Crawl in here and sleep as long as you want. There is plenty of soap and towels in the shower. The kitchen is always open and plenty of food when you get hungry."

He grinned and looked at the floor. "You're the best friend I have. The only friend I have."

"I can't believe that, honey." Her arms drew him near. "Promise you'll be here when it gets dark."

He nodded. "Promise."

At the foot of the stairs, the sound of Turk's voice drifted out from his office. He sounded angry, his voice low but icy. That was probably what she should expect from now on.

Not yet ready to confront him about Shane's unannounced arrival, she slipped out the door and stood on the patio. The sun cast long afternoon shadows across the yard. Blissful silence was pierced by an argument between several Blue Jays darting from limb to limb in a nearby Spruce tree.

"What are you doing out here?"

Turk stood only inches from her and she hadn't been aware of his presence until now. She spun to face him, heart in her throat.

"You frightened me."

"I meant to."

So, here they were, back to their former snapping and biting relationship. Why he was so distant now escaped her, but accepting his mood would be best all around.

The real reason for his aloof attitude was better left un-tampered with. *But, no. You never were patient, no matter how the truth might hurt.*

"Turk." She knotted the sash of her robe. "When you want to talk civilly, I'd be glad to hear why you're so upset and cold."

He gripped her upper arm in the old, impersonal, angry way. "You're babbling again. Get in the house."

"I'm calling my grandmother, like it or not." She slapped at his hand. "You can go play with you gun."

Here she was, playing with fire again.

"Huffy." He lowered his head to speak quietly in her ear, soft Texas drawl iced over with the monotone delivery. "You're not going to do anything I don't okay first. Got that?"

"Excuse me." She tapped his chest with a chipped nail. "Are you the same man that served sex for lunch on the kitchen table, or the prick that I first met here at the lodge?"

Well, that was stupid. The truth wasn't what she really wanted. She'd made a mistake, letting him have her only asset. Now she had no card to deal.

Brushing past him didn't work. His reflex was fast and his hand strong, catching her arm to stop her.

"I never stopped being that prick." He eyed her with slow deliberation, looking down the gaping collar of her robe. "I'd rather you wore clothes around here."

Flouncing her shoulder at him, she pulled the robe close about her, neck to thigh. "That's strange. It never bothered you before. Don't you worry your pinhead about my clothes. You won't be seeing me anytime soon after tonight."

Turk grimaced with a familiar expression of aggravation, his jaw clenched and eyes looking to heaven. "Sorry, Toots, but you're coming in here with me and I'll tell you what you'll be doing from now on."

No question about it, he was right and she walked on tiptoe beside him into the house. His strength held her up until her toes only grazed the polished oak floors of the house. He slammed the door to the office after he hauled her inside.

"Shhh. You'll wake Shane!"

He didn't look at her and she was grateful for that. His shoulders squared, accentuating his male presence. She caught the scent of his cologne, and it mixed like an aphrodisiac with his male suppressed anger to her senses.

"Don't tempt me to throw him out to the wolves." Turk pointed to a chair. "Sit. Stay awhile."

"I don't have time."

"That's all you have."

"No, I still have my good sense and it's telling me to get the hell away from you."

He lit a cigar, dropping into his squeaky desk chair to gaze at her. The turquoise hue of his eyes deepened with his brief smile. "Stop the drama stuff." He puffed several times on the cigar. "I've heard it all."

What did that mean? That he'd had a lot of other women begging for his help? Okay, we'll play games. She loosened her belt, taking the chair near the desk.

"There you go again, playing the snarling beast." Her robe fell open, exposing her legs to the upper thigh.

She gasped with surprise as he hooked his foot in the last rung of her chair, snapping her around to face him. "Now. I'm not the kind of guy that can play games or pretend I don't want to fuck you. You know that would be a lie."

She tried to get up, but he stopped her with a hand to her shoulder. Her temper flared. "Turk. Your sexual appetite is of no interest to me. You have no intent of offering a helping hand to either me or Shane."

Tiny glints of green fire awakened in his narrowed gaze. "The punk is still alive only because you seem to think he's the man to make your dreams come true. Don't spoil it for him with your smart assed remarks."

Abigail relaxed in her chair. He grabbed a handful of the rainbow colored jellybeans from the cut glass candy dish, tossing most of them in his mouth. He didn't put the lid on the fancy dish, helping himself to a second handful.

She couldn't help it if the collar of her robe opened and the silky fabric wandered off her shoulder. His gaze touched her bare skin with hunger flaring wild and hot. Scenes from their hot tryst made her wet with remembered taste of his lips after he'd licked her breasts clean.

She reached into the candy dish, popping a succulent lilac piece in her mouth. She didn't chew. Only sucked the sweet flavor off the morsel. Through the narrowed slits of her eyes, she observed him, his intent study of everything she did. He licked his lips before turning away.

"I was serious about the clothes."

"I seriously don't care."

He gripped the arms of her chair, glaring into her eyes as he threw papers over her head. "Damn you, Huffy." His face flushed with tightly coiled emotions. "That's the last communication I got from my brother in Dallas. He can't come out here to take you off my hands because he leads a normal fucking life."

"Don't try to flatter me with sweet nothings." Slapping papers from the desk, she stood, ignoring her errant robe. "If he's as evil as you, it's best he stays in Dallas."

"Shut up." The sharp command startled her. "You didn't read the last bit on your friend. His job as a mule for an enemy of the United States has been queered. What's he told you about this?"

Breathing wasn't easy with all the horrible weight of his news sitting on her chest. "He said he didn't know what he was into, that he threw the briefcase in some weeds near the office building where he got it."

"Bullshit." Standing tall and angry, he glanced at her over his shoulder. "Here's what's been going on. He got away from the Arab and he's running with the stuff they stole." He worked his shoulders as if his back ached. "Gun says the Fed's lost Kufu and the boy would probably get lost on the road. That was supposed to be funny."

"Shane told me everything. He doesn't lie!"

The glint of supreme 'I told you so' shot daggers through her. "What?"

"He doesn't lie."

"That's what I thought you said." She jumped and stifled a scream when he smashed his fist into the sturdy walnut wardrobe. "Then explain to me why you're sitting here when we all know you have a much better life waiting in the UK?"

Defending her friend just became a lot more difficult.

"Okay. Things didn't go exactly as planned, but he didn't cause any of my problems."

He grew quiet, hooking his thumbs in the belt loops of his jeans. "Damn, Huffy. He'll never know he's not worth your spit."

Chapter 17

The house was quiet, like Christmas Eve at home when he was a kid. Turk lay in his leather recliner listening, recognizing every soft moan and creak of well-aged lumber around him.

With Huffy upstairs comforting Wonder Boy, trying to keep his imagination in check was impossible. He glanced at the ceiling before reaching for the novel he'd found on the coffee table. It was about two men and one woman. Pretty damn ironic.

He couldn't stop thinking about Huffy, and the way she'd run to make Shane comfortable. How long had she been up there?

You damn fool. She'll probably stay with him. He's more her type anyway. And a hell of a lot younger.

Shane was everything he wasn't. Carefree to the point of stupid, and cocksure with Huffy.

The icy wind was coming straight down from the mountains, funneling through the canyon above the ranch. Turk wondered why he'd left the warmth of Dallas for this cold son-of-a-bitch.

He got up to close the bedroom window, and peered out at the inky darkness. He'd never seen a place so dark at night. Unless it had been in the desert. But, that was no mans land. This was his place. Maybe he'd look into some outdoor lighting.

Stop complaining, fool. You're just pissed off because you didn't satisfy her.

What the hell could he do about that? His ass hurt along with the wrenching pain of stress in his gut.

He needed a shot of Jack Black.

His luck was running pretty even tonight. The whiskey decanter on the library table was empty. That meant a trip to the kitchen. If he met Huffy out there, she'd think he was spying on her. *Damn.*

He turned away from the window, gritting his teeth over a groan of pain, and hobbled to the kitchen with no concern about looking weak.

He winced, taking in the condition of the room. Dishes and food littered the table and floor. The place looked like a wild roadhouse.

Hell with it. Plenty of time to clean up tomorrow. Right now, the bottle of good whiskey on the sideboard called to him.

He grabbed the bottle and took a bowl of fresh strawberries from the refrigerator.

Drink and sustenance. What a fucked up life.

The pain in his hip was of such proportions he couldn't ignore it any longer or the warm trickle of blood from the wound. Just a painful reminder of being a first class dick-head trying to get cozy with Huffy.

Out in the entry hall, he clamped his teeth on his bottom lip to stop the yelp of pain after smacking his toe against the leg of the rocker by the door.

He checked the door one more time, giving in to the urge to look up the staircase. Wanting Huffy in a way that he couldn't put a name to had begun to mess with his mind. Thinking like that was dangerous.

Okay, you're jealous. He'd never been jealous of another human being before, but he'd never connected with a woman with such powerful emotions.

He had to face facts, that he didn't want Huffy to leave him, especially not with another man. He'd dared think about the two of them later down the road, married and him teaching her to ride western style. How to whip up a first rate chili. There'd been a couple of dark haired kids in that daydream. That didn't sound pussy when he said it in his head.

It would be hell to have Huffy catch him mooning over her in the hall. He made it to his room, closing the door before cursing under his breath.

He put the snack items on the nightstand before stripping off his threadbare sweats, and then turned on the water. The shower spray stung and made the damn wound bleed harder.

There was something odd about the lighting in the bathroom now that he was out of the shower and drying his aching body. Hell fire, another bulb burned out.

A shadow fell across the steamed up mirror, and his heart pounded with surprise. The sweet fragrance of warm lilac's drifted around him. He leaned against the vanity for support.

"Did you forget something?" *Lame. So damn lame.*

"Don't you want me here?"

Her sweet face was all he could see for a few seconds, and the way she reached out to press her palm to his burning hip. She stepped beside him, meeting his gaze with no sign of wanting to leave.

"What a question." He dropped his towel and brushed his fingers along her jaw. "I've been waiting for you."

She glanced down at the blood on her palm, her contrite expression jolting his nerves. "I would never purposely hurt you, Turk."

His heart squeezed, near exploding just hearing her say his name without adding a cuss word to it. "I know that. This was my fault."

His manly words were ignored, and she hugged his waist before looking through the medicine cabinet.

"Antiseptic?" She whispered her question so sweetly, he wanted to whine like a baby.

"Behind the box of floss."

She showed real proficiency with a roll of gauze and tape, using the tiny scissors to make a bandage for him.

He could have taken a rocket to the head with no problem as she knelt behind him, her delicate fingers working on his tough-as-leather ass. The antiseptic burned a little, but she blew on it and his dick shot straight up against his belly.

He jumped, his glutes hard as rocks where she soothed them, rubbing her cool palm over them. No argument from him. His blood was too hot for conversation now that she pressed her lips to his torn up flesh before securing the bandage.

She stood up, smiling at him in the mirror. The woman ripped his heart out just by being this close to him. Did she know that? If he could ever breathe normally again, he'd tell her how he felt.

This was too much for him to live through. She slipped her arm around his waist and took his throbbing cock in her hand, squeezing and working her fingers up and down the hot flesh. The veins stood up and ran full with sizzling blood, keeping him hard as gunmetal.

He opened his eyes to see her bathrobe drop to the floor. A moment later, there was the gentle warmth of her breath against his shoulder, followed by the exquisite sensation of her bare breasts against his tense back.

When she spoke, he wanted to tattoo the sound in his memory, to keep it close forever. "I think we need to go to bed."

Wake up fool. It's not a dream. Say something and please let it be clever.

"Huffy." He turned to pull her into his arms, breathing hard, trying not to pressure her. "My bed's real close."

"Uh-hm." He came undone when her soft arms went about his neck. "That's the one I meant."

The kiss wouldn't wait. Turk held her face in his hands to take her moist lips in an orgiastic kiss that touched and tasted every pulse and curve of her lush mouth.

She did what he'd been wet dreaming about. Gasping with passion and hooking her leg over his thigh to move against him.

"Turk, do we need jelly tonight?"

His chuckle was just pure nerves and never before experienced delight. "I'll get the whole damn kitchen if that's what you want, baby."

* * * *

Abigail had never wanted him so much. Tonight he was being so tender and it went straight to her pounding heart.

He lifted her, taking her to his massive bed to carefully lay her down. "The lamp, Turk. I want to see you."

She flicked her tongue over her lips, a hunger for him raising her most forbidden desire, the decadent needs sharpened by the lamp's soft illumination. He was a gloriously strong man, every hard contour bathed in the warm glow of lamplight. Lean muscles bathed in a warm golden hue heightened his male desirability. He was erect and, ready to take her to the climax she'd thought about all day.

She wanted more than that, a lot more. Her heart beat wildly in welcome as he dropped down to lay with her. The kiss that started in the bathroom began all over again and she opened her mouth to welcome his exploring tongue.

He tasted of sex, whetting her appetite for fun. "Want to play a game, Cowboy?" She smiled at his puzzled expression. "The rules easy and extremely enjoyable."

He stood, pouring a shot glass full of Black Jack and dropped a handful of berries in the amber liquid. "I make my own rules." He placed the glass on her stomach and smiled wolfishly at her. "Open your legs, Gorgeous."

His husky command sent a ripple of anticipation through her body. Her thighs eased apart without hesitation. "I think I'm going to like your game."

"Well, we'll keep playing until you do, my wild Arizona rose."

"You made up a new name for me." She closed her eyes, shivering while her body quickened under his finger circling her nipples. "I love it."

His eyes were beautiful, warm and sexy. "Don't move. I have more to show you."

No answer, no sir. He was doing a bang up job of driving her crazy, accidentally brushing her nipple, licking Jack from her breasts on his way down to plop a berry in her navel, then held it in his fingers to slip it into her opening.

He smiled wolfishly, then bent to lap the liquid from her belly button.

Her soft laughter blended into a gasp of raw pleasure while he dripped juice over her mounds and went on to dip his tongue into her sensitive, wet slit.

"You've done this before." She caught his hair in her fingers, holding his mouth to her quivering belly. Her every expectation was coming to fruition now, the secret out as pushed her hand away and moved down to breathe on her pulsing lips, nuzzling the ruby folds.

She could only muster a moan of absolute surrender.

He brought her pure bliss, indescribable pleasure danced over her skin with every brush of his tongue playing around her nub. She bit her lip, holding back the scream of ecstasy while his nibbled the strawberry that moved against her already aroused flesh.

Juice trickled between her lips to be slowly sipped and sucked away. Heat coursed dangerously through her body, her limbs quivering beneath his seeking lips.

She didn't try to silence the cry of delight as his tongue touched to her slit, darting in to taste her with an expertise she'd never question him about.

He dangled the erotic fire of orgasm just out of reach, grazing her sensitized bud with his long fingers, driving her closer to the release she desired. He touched her clit, moving up to fit himself between her thighs.

"Let me." She moaned softly, jolted by the heat and weight of his cock in her hand. Her legs opened and hips thrust up to take all of him, greedy for his warmth and weight that would make her completely his.

While her emotions raged, Abigail wasn't sure she would live through the torrid heat consuming her or survive the ecstasy of his touch, the strength of his arms and hands that caressed with such tender seduction.

She drank in his scent of lotus and cedar, memorized the texture of his olive hued muscles and the strong contours of his strong back and arms.

She loved him, needed him and wanted to make him love her. If sex were the only thing she had to offer, she'd make him want her forever.

Right now, he seemed too wrapped in passion to ever stop, his lips taking hers in deep, demanding kisses that urged her to the fire and pulled her in, the liquid heat sweeping her in a Babylonian, sobbing climax.

Her senses were slow to release the memory of their joyful climb to the stratosphere. How could she ever convince herself there would be other visits to that sultry Avalon?

He made her fly, and her blood sang as he lifted her to his chest in his orgasm, lifting her off the bed as if she were precious to him.

She wanted to make him feel it too, but couldn't speak, only melted into the inferno of their lovemaking.

Chapter 18

Abigail hadn't given a thought to the morning after, or had time to rehearse a sexy greeting for the moment they first opened their eyes.

That would have been a waste of time. Turk wasn't lolling in the sheets as she'd expected. She was alone.

This was a ranch after all, and he was a rancher. Thank God for cowboys.

At the foot of the bed lay a pair of faded jeans and a threadbare white cotton shirt. All clean and comfy like the man who'd put them there.

She crawled out of the blissfully soft quilts and dragged the clothing with her to the shower. The tile was still damp from Turk's shower, the scent of his soap and aftershave teasing her into a moment of self-indulgence.

This must be his soap, a saddle shaped handful of sensual aroma. Holding it under the spray, she inhaled the scent of Turk, then slid the soap over her breasts, shivering with the insatiable need that he alone could quench. Even his soap left her nipples hard and tingling with an eager pulse.

That was so exquisite, the rest of her body deserved some playtime. She leaned against the tile while rubbing the bar over her stomach and down her tense thighs. Bubbles played over her skin and hurried down her legs, some forming a lovely dam of fragrant foam between her legs.

Oh, my god, the caress of the bar to her sensitized folds sent her into orbit, small tremors of orgasm jerking her forward to hug the wall.

Stop it, you alley cat. Go find him. You want him to touch you.

She bathed quickly, anxious to be with him. The towels were king sized and slightly rough, just like Turk. Her thoughts pulled her back to the ecstasy of the night before, the way his lips and hands had sent her spiraling off to delightful places she'd never been.

With her hair dried and neatly bound into a single braid, she pulled on the clean smelling garments she'd hung from hooks on the door.

The jeans were too long but she folded the legs up several times to make adjustments. She tied the shirt in a loose knot at her waist, quickly falling in love with the comfortable way it cuddled her ribcage and breasts.

She found a worn leather belt in his closet and worked it through the loops of the jeans. It was soft, and easily gave in to the scissors she used to make the belt fit.

Eager to be with Turk, she followed the aroma of bacon and eggs, hungry as a wolf after such an active night.

That hunger escalated to ravenous as her gaze settled on the man loading the dishwasher.

You're crazy for him, Abigail, but does he really look better each time you see him? Silly woman, you know he does. Remembering the way he loved her all night long weakened her knees.

He straightened and grinned at her. It hadn't been her imagination working while they'd had sex. His mouth had literally taken her through the pages of Karma Sutra and on to Sheherezade's tent.

You've become such a hot pants, her nagging woman's voice chided with a snicker. Laughing at the truth of the comment, she dipped her hands in the pockets of her oversized jeans.

"Good morning, tall, dark and unbelievable in bed."

"That was nothing." He dried his hands on the towel stuffed in the waist of his jeans. "Just an appetizer." He pulled her close to brush his lips across hers.

"I'm not busy right now, cowboy." Her craving spun out of control, every nerve bristling with need. "My God, you can't get any harder...or can you?"

"I can and will."

Life was so good at that moment Abigail trembled with joy as well as worry.

He picked her up, looking into her eyes with such desire, the power of it stung her heart. How would she ever go back to the life she'd known before Turk?

Stop being a fool. Take what life hands you. Right now, it has handed you the once in a lifetime man.

"Hey, you two." Shane eyed them with a knowing smile from the doorway. "I'll work for food."

Abigail didn't want Shane to see the painful disappointment in her eyes. Her laugh sounded cheerful, but her crestfallen mood lay heavy after being forced back to reality.

Turk put her down, his body tensed with unsatisfied desire. "It's on the table, Shane. We'll talk work later."

"I don't guess I could work out enough money for two plane tickets to Britain?" Shane was unaware of the bristle in Turk's expression, while he looked hungrily at the bacon on his plate.

"You know anything about horses, Shane?"

"Sure."

"Like what?"

"I've been to the track. I know how the bookies work."

Turk choked on his coffee. "No, I mean the care of the animals."

"Oh, sure." Confidence poured from Shane. "You feed them a lot...don't you?"

"You can. If you want fat horses." Turk's voice lowered an octave. "How'd you get that name?"

"My parents." Shane shrugged lightly. "They love western movies."

"Nothing wrong with that." Turk moved the peppershaker closer to the hungry young man. "It's a good name."

Surprise registered on Shane's face. "Thanks." He grinned and tucked his chin after forking more egg into his mouth. "I'll hurry and we can go see about the herd."

Abigail listened to the interaction between the men, allowing herself to linger on the sweetness of the moment, and the passion that had taken place in Turk's bed, and on this very table.

Abigail caught Turk's quick smile. Oh, yes, this was going to work out after all.

She tore her gaze from his face to look at Shane as he made plans for them.

"I'm trying to work out enough for our plane tickets to Puerto Vallarta and on to England. Turk's a fair man. He'll help us out."

The knot in her chest was her heart, the beat thudding to a stop after Shane's pronouncement. "I'm sure things will work out." She put her cup down, startled by Turk's abrupt movement as he left the table.

"Let's go earn some of that money, fella." Turk walked behind her chair, grazing her neck with his fingertip.

The flush of passion flamed through her. Disguising her emotions took Herculean effort.

"I'll just go find my shoes and go with you."

He arched a brow, inclining his head toward the back door. "What? You don't want to wear my boots anymore?"

"Don't be silly." Somehow, she'd forgotten her high flying plans and why she'd been so miserable. His smile was magic. "I'll run up and get them."

He winked at her and reached for his hat where it hung from a peg on the door. "I'll wait."

Will you, my darling?

The future she'd risked all for no longer seemed important. Could he see the tumbling emotion in her eyes? She hoped so.

What a difference a day makes.

Turk's pleasant thought accompanied the reeling sensation of being just plain stupid happy.

He kept his hands busy while she was gone, checking the ammo in his .45 and dropping another clip in his pocket.

"I'm ready," came the sweet call from his woman.

God almighty, listen to yourself.

"Me too, baby." He'd thought he knew every facet of her face, but when he got a close up of her lips, rockets exploded in his boxers.

This was so powerful and so good. Off in the distance a warning sign blinked…slow…slow…slower. Everything comes to an end.

Footsteps in the hall affirmed the fact he was living a dream.

He stopped Shane's eager attempt at opening the door. "Hold it. I'll go out first. Huffy, you walk between me and Shane Boy." The sudden light of fear in her eyes softened his attitude. "Just stay close. Okay?"

"I'm not scared." She looked at Shane as if making sure he understood the situation. "Let's go."

They quick-stepped along the path to the stable. Long fingers of golden sunlight crossed the narrow walkway.

The morning was the kind Turk liked. Quiet, except for late summer crickets singing in the dry, sweet grass. He reached behind him to make sure Huffy was close. She gripped his fingers to confirm she was within reach.

His nerves settled down once they were inside the stable. The horses waited at the door of their stalls, ready for grain and the freedom of the pasture.

"Okay." Turk took Huffy to the tack room. "You stay put while we take care of the horses."

"I'll start mucking."

Her words made him laugh. "Wait until I get back." He brushed his lips across hers, and inhaled roughly.

He had only a second to see the unfolding scene before chaos took over. Shane had opened all the stalls and now the animals stampeded through the doors, busting for outside and freedom.

"Aw, damn it!"

More trouble rained down on Shane when he tried to fix his mistake and ran in front of the herd. Turk yelled at him, but his warning came too late. Brushed aside by a galloping wave of horseflesh, Shane was thrown against a support beam and lay flat, and silent.

Over the furor, he heard Huffy's scream. He'd hoped to spare her another moment of trauma, but here he was, causing more of the same.

Waving his warms to turn the herd, he raced toward Shane where he lay gasping for breath. The roar subsided and Huffy was a blur running past him.

They knelt to check out the wheezing young man. Shane slowly sat up, a crooked grin on his bloody face. Huffy was doing it again, sobbing over the idiot kid and wiping his face with the old shirt he'd given her.

"Shane, please talk to me." Her tears dropped onto the kid's bloody face making trails down his lean cheek. He had the balls to laugh and make a goofy remark after what he'd done.

"I got em outside."

"Yeah." Turk shook his head. "You just forgot to feed them." He quickly wet a clean cloth and wiped the blood from Shane's face. This fiasco brought back the harsh events of his last detail in the Middle East. "Just a bloody nose. Want to go back to the house?"

"No way. I'm earning my money here."

Turk stopped Shane from running after the horses. "They'll be all right for now. Grab a shovel and start cleaning stalls." He eyed Shane with new respect. The kid was impossible to dislike, a rambunctious colt.

He walked Huffy to a nail keg. "Sit until we finish here." Fear lingered in her eyes and her hands still trembled. "I won't be long."

He went back to work, hurrying to get them out of the stable. It didn't feel right to him, to be away from the house and the phones. Damn, he should have brought one out.

Taking in Shane's appearance, Turk felt pretty small for being tough on him. The guy's clothes were in shreds, and he needed a haircut. Easy enough to take care of.

He tossed a handful of straw at Huffy where she sat waiting for him. "Okay, people. As soon as we finish up here, we're all going to Blue Bears."

From his stall at the back of the stable, Shane gave a darn authentic sounding, "Yee-Haw."

Huffy's face brightened. "Really? I'd love that."

"I'm here to please." He questioned the motive behind her easy agreement, but thought better of it. Especially after her soft reply.

"And you certainly do that," her whisper as beautiful as she was.

A nagging worry tugged his gut. He was too happy. Something was bound to fuck it up. After he shoveled out several stalls, he paused to look at her.

He was being stupid. The most beautiful, desirable woman sat in his smelly stable, thumbing through a veterinary records book.

Turk grimaced, resisting cold, hard truth. Had he become such a basket case, he couldn't face the truth? What made him think she'd toss her life aside for him?

How long would Huffy be happy with that kind of entertainment? He knew what was coming. She'd get bored, she'd want bright lights, party's, and crowds. He didn't plan to ever leave Lone Horse. But could he for Huffy?

Chapter 19

They drove with the windows down and shared coffee from a large, dented, silver thermos on the way to Blue Bear's. Seated between Turk and Shane, Abigail popped in a CD and country rock made it a party.

"Do they sell nail polish at Blue Bear's?" Her question hadn't seemed outrageous, yet Turk's arched brows and grin said it had been. "Well, do they?"

"We'll ask." He leaned his shoulder against her, the move pressing his solid body to hers, his warmth seeping through the fine material of her jacket.

His mood changed slightly after their truck rolled past a parked RV that was partially hidden by the drooping limbs of an old pine. The RV appeared to be a late model, definitely not abandoned.

Turk glanced across the cab at Shane. "That your ride back there?"

"Naw. I left mine up on the four lane." Shane looked a little uncomfortable, but covered it with a laugh. "My wheels were an old van I borrowed from my…last employer."

Abigail couldn't believe Turk had laughed at Shane's colorful words. Tension invaded the small space.

"Does that RV mean trouble?" She shivered with a fierce wave of worry.

"Probably not." Turk glanced at her before checking the rearview mirror. "Could be a fisherman or a guy looking for a place to be alone with his girl."

"Then, they were probably in the van." She nodded and gave his thigh a light tap.

She loved his sexy grin. Maybe he thought they should be doing the same thing.

The ride went quickly and they arrived at Blue Bear's, finding a parking slot near the back entrance.

They piled out and headed for the door. Abigail used a dusty display window to check her appearance. Not too bad for a gal who hadn't seen a spa or facial in weeks. Matter of fact, she had a damn good glow on.

She'd changed into a sleeveless, buttercup yellow suit with a mini skirt. She felt liberated wearing no stockings with her white kidskin pumps. If Turk's warming glances to her bare legs meant anything, she had chosen well.

The memory of her first visit to this place flashed through her brain, the way that woman had touched him.

He pressed his hand to her waist and opened the door, the smile on his lips speaking loud and clear what was on his mind. He leaned closer to whisper against her ear. "Don't forget who brought you to the dance."

Abigail loved him for his sweet joke. "Don't you know I'm saving the last dance for you?"

From behind them, Shane grunted with impatience. "Come on you guy's. I want a beer."

Turk held Shane back for a second. "You old enough to drink?"

"You have to be kidding. I'm older than Abbey. I used to buy drinks for her before she had her last birthday."

The guy never knew when to shut up. "That'll be enough, Shane." She gave him a warning glare and went inside the hazy back room. "You men go ahead with whatever you were going to do. I want to shop around."

Turk pointed to the door with a painted figure of a cowgirl on it. "The ladies room if you need it."

"Thanks." His concern for her comfort was quite a pleasant change from their early relationship. She remembered all the heated disagreements and her deliberate acts to provoke him. Now all she wanted was to be with him.

Don't make too much of it. He's a gentleman.

Turk and Shane went to the room off to the side where men's clothing was stacked on tables and wall shelves. She stood in the doorway to look around.

Hats of every style and description hung from pegs on the walls, and rows of hatboxes were stacked high on the floor. Sturdy looking shirts and jackets were displayed on racks near the door that led to the bar. This had to be where Turk bought his clothes. She shot a whimsical glance toward him.

Not a tux in sight.

The boot display sported a mishmash of colors and designs. If she was to help Turk in the stable, she probably needed a pair.

She moved down the aisle and inspected the smaller sized footwear. Something about the gleaming soft leather with hand tooled flowers struck her fancy.

The price tag stunned her. Two hundred and fifty dollars to be exact.

Well, you have nowhere to go. Try them on.

Tossing her finely made pumps aside, Abigail pulled the boots on. They hugged her feet and lifted her up an inch and a half. She walked up and down the narrow space between racks and grinned.

You're a boob. Put them back.

"Hi. They look good."

Abigail's head jerked up with a start. That woman was standing there, eyeing her with a slight smile. "Thanks. Just trying them on." Memories of the way Glenda had ground herself into Turk's crotch stirred the embers of resentment in Abigail. "You work here, don't you?"

"I tend bar at night." She adjusted her bra straps. "That's when the action starts."

"I see."

Tempering her tongue, Abigail removed the boots and put them back in their box. Glenda didn't leave, simply stared at her with open curiosity before speaking again.

"Bertha said you were Turk's favorite at the ranch."

Abigail's heart hammered in her chest. "I'm glad to hear he likes me." Stepping into her pumps, she gestured toward her companion. "Did Bertha tell you everything she did?"

Backing up several steps to allow Abigail to leave, Glenda laughed softly. "She said you're scared of horses and anything that moved. Playing games with you gave her a big laugh."

"She was probably right." Why hadn't she been smart enough to see what Bertha was up to? "Pretty funny, huh? What else did she pull?"

Lighting a super long cigarette, Glenda guffawed. "She liked to sneak off up in the hills and smoke. Her and one of the local ranch boys that needed tutoring. They spent lots of time up in those pine trees."

So, Bertha had been the cause of many dirty looks she'd gotten from Turk. "I don't suppose she told you about the cell phone she left in my room?" Abigail swatted her hip and laughed. "Just too funny."

With her icy veneer thawed enough to be friendly, Glenda grinned. "She knew Turk would go off on you like a buzz saw over a phone. We drank a full bottle of wine on that one."

Feeling a little crushed to know someone disliked her that much, Abigail looked past the talkative woman. "I'd better go. The men are probably waiting for me." Closing the lid down on the boot box, she smiled at Glenda. "It was nice meeting you."

Grinding her smoke on the floor, Glenda nodded. "Same here." She started out the side door, but hesitated. "Me and Turk were never anything serious. He's a great guy and has always been nice to me. Sorry Bertha was such a bitch to you."

Abigail watched as she disappeared behind the racks then listened for the squeak of the closing door. The need to be with Turk consumed her, and she hurried back to the other side of the store.

Somehow, Glenda made it to the men's clothing before Abigail. Turk sorted through a stack of chambray shirts while Glenda flirted with Shane. He didn't seem to mind, hugging his newfound friend and moving several feet away to hold a private conversation.

He'd always drawn women with no trouble and Glenda wasted no time in roping him in.

Soft music from the jukebox was the finishing touch and in a blink, the two of them were in a hot embrace on the dance floor.

Now Abigail knew why their relationship had never gone beyond friend. He was a kid, willing to play games with all comers.

Her gaze went to the man she wanted with every breath she took. Tall, strong and decent was the message Turk sent out, and she wanted to be close as possible to him.

"Hi." Abigail stood close to him, bumping her hip to his. "What's good today?"

He dropped his hand down to pat her rear. "I'd say I found it."

With a familiarity reserved for couples in love, she slipped her fingers into his back pocket. "How long is this going to take?"

"No longer than absolutely necessary."

Previously masked desire burned free and hot in his glance, his mouth opening slightly for the deliberate slide of his tongue that moistened his lips.

Maybe he needed some extra incentive.

"No hurry, cowboy." She slid her hand into his pocket to press his thigh. "But, I know where the orange liquor is kept."

"Well, if that's not reason to hurry home, I don't know what is." He leaned close to murmur in her ear. "Did you get that fingernail stuff you wanted?"

Abigail shook her head and smiled at her thoughtful man. "No, I had a talk with Glenda, and completely forgot."

His brows shifted up ever so slightly. Abigail stifled a laugh. *Why make it too easy on him? Let the cowboy explain how it had been with the two of them.*

He didn't say a word. Smart man.

Turk eyed her with an assessing gaze, touched her jaw with his knuckles before picking up several shirts for Shane.

What was Huffy up to? It wasn't as if he had anything to hide, but hopefully Glenda hadn't been too colorful describing their relationship.

Inside the bar, the lights were dim and lent a more private feel to the place. Turk ordered two longnecks and handed one of the cold brews to Huffy. Something else he hadn't expected as she turned it up and took a long drink.

Damn, she kept giving him her secretive, sidelong look, turning her head as if she was laughing. The trophy elk head over the bar made him think he should be up there, because he was good as bagged and tagged.

"Huffy." He tapped her shoulder. "You might as well tell me what Glenda told you."

She leaned against him, touching his knuckles with her fingertip. "Don't get a big head, but she thinks you're a nice guy."

He took a long drink, looking at her over the bottle. "That's it?"

"Pretty much."

Obviously, Huffy wanted to play games, and he wanted to go home. Where was that kid? Out on the dance floor, Glenda and Shane wrapped around each other to the beat of a romantic country ballad.

Turk had thought right about the baby-face kid being the kind women went for. Looking at Huffy, he wanted her in his arms, and yes by damn, dance with her.

Aw hell. No time for that. A brawl erupted at the far end of the bar, and he wanted no part of it. He pushed Huffy down to keep her from being hit by a hurtling beer bottle. She screamed as a flying missile crashed into the mirror behind them to spatter beer over everything within ten feet.

She raised her head to watch the action with the same glow in her eyes he'd seen every time trouble arrived. She was a dangerous woman and he liked it. Hell, this was no good.

She grabbed his sleeve and squeezed her eyes shut when the two cursing men landed on the floor at their feet. The juke box went right on playing, and the bartender cussed, trying to pry the men apart, his only question asking who was going to pay for the damage.

Reality hammered at the walls of the Eden he'd found himself in. What had happened to his head?

He'd let his dick get in the way of what he knew best. Vigilance. His mood abruptly changed from lovesick hound dog to wary Doberman.

"Come on." He lifted her over the drunken warriors on the floor and walked rapidly toward the exit. "We'll pick up Shane on our way out."

Of course she'd been startled. The look in her blue eyes said she was a little afraid of his gruff attitude. *Damn it.*

She bit her lip and looked down as he hurried her from the place, not saying a word as he helped her into the truck. He could see Shane's look of question as he got in to sit beside her.

Turk secured the supplies in the back, glancing through the window at the couple in the cab. Oh, hell yes, he'd ruined the mood and didn't have a tinker's damn of an idea how to repair it.

While he covered the baskets of early fall apples and peaches Blue Bear had loaded in the back of the truck with a tarp, he considered his position. He had to be ready for trouble when it came, and it would. Mooning over the one he was supposed to be protecting was way out of line. Caught with his pants down meant they would all probably die. Horny or not, he'd keep his dick in his shorts.

He was getting too domestic. Hell, if things didn't straighten up around here, he'd be knitting socks for the damn horses.

He slammed the tailgate shut and wished he could erase the last few months of his life. What he felt for Huffy went far beyond sex and he was fooling himself about the rosy future that had become a frequent visitor in his dreams.

Chapter 20

Turk's mood changed from flirty charmer to wary abrasiveness. He was worried about her and Shane. She'd instigated this silent atmosphere and that put a crushing guilt on her heart.

Most of the speed limit signs were rusted out and riddled with bullet holes—but she was pretty sure Turk was far exceeding the speed limit. He took the sharp curves without slowing down, prompting her to grip his thigh to stay on the seat.

"Buckle up."

"You're not."

"Just do it."

Okay. To avoid a scene, she fastened her seatbelt and wished the tense aura would vanish.

Turk smoked a cigar as he drove and avoided looking at her. Even Shane seemed withdrawn and nervous.

Once they arrived home, Turk practically carried her to the front door, and kept her close as he made a quick check of the house.

The two men she truly loved were at high risk, caught in the fray, and certainly in line to die at the hands of a mad man. All because she'd been too needy and ignorant of the facts of life. Shane got himself in hot water trying to help her. He was repaid with the possibility of being killed for his kindness. If they came out of this situation in good standing, she'd try to make it up to them.

She wept silently. Was Turk ever to feel anything but disgust for her?

Stop being a fool, Abigail. He had you and that was all you had to offer. You gave more than your body away this time. Your heart was in that ribbon bedecked gift.

"Huffy!"

Turk yelled her name, and her heart fluttered against her ribs.

"Yes." Her voice crackled, the sound like stepping on thin ice. "I'm out here."

"Come in here." There was an icy pause. "I have something to say."

That could only mean he'd gotten another fax from his brother.

She tried to make herself as small as possible, scrunching her shoulders as she walked into the office and stood waiting at the door. "What is it?" He leaned over the desk and roughed his hair.

His cool glance and hard grimace left no doubt he wasn't interested in a petting session. She'd pissed him off and now stood in his line of fire.

"Kufu Fa was seen in Santa Fe."

What did that mean? She didn't care to risk questioning him. Turk circled a paragraph on the fax sheet.

"What are we going to do?"

He pushed away from the desk and went to the liquor cabinet. The set of his jaw as he poured a whiskey, and the way he swallowed a healthy gulp confirmed something dreadful was in their future.

"What we're going to do is be ready." He pointed to the gun collection displayed in a glass case on the wall. "They're all loaded and when the time comes, you'll use one."

"I can't!"

"You will." The thought terrified her. He'd probably call her a coward, but she'd rather hide until the danger had gone away. Her trembling hands should tell him that.

"What about Shane?" Her lip bled from her nervous bite. "He isn't military. He knows nothing about guns."

"I already had a chat with Shane. He knows what to do."

"And what's that?" She'd never been so close to fainting from fear. "Why do we have to act like savages?"

He turned, pinning her with the fury and ice in his gaze. "I thought you were smarter." He moved closer, leaning into her as he set the shot glass on the desk. "We're not the savages here. On the offside chance he takes both me and Shane out, he'll look for any one alive. He doesn't leave witnesses." His voice was gravely as he described the horrific possibilities. "Am I making myself clear?"

She froze, the savage words forming images she didn't want to see.

He didn't move, his gaze burning into hers.

Her mouth went dry. "Can't we hide somewhere?"

"He's bringing the fight to me. I won't be driven off my own land."

How could she have been so naïve? This man lived by the code of the old west.

He stared at her exactly as he would have a spineless varmint.

"You're not even close, lady."

Did he have any idea how badly she felt? Not a chance. He looked at her through new eyes, and her ease of crawling into his bunk didn't help her cause any.

"Okay, I can see that nothing I say will change anything."

She turned to leave, but he blocked the door with his arm. "I'm trying to keep you alive. Don't make the job any harder than necessary."

This was good a time as any to make her pitch for understanding and maybe a start on righting things between them. "I have something to say and I want you to hear me out."

"I'm listening." Was he? Not really, not with the closed look in his eyes and the determined set of his jaw.

"I'll do whatever you say. But, first I want you to know I admit to being the cause of all this. I can't take it back and restart the clock. I'm sorry for messing up your perfect life."

He didn't move a muscle, merely looked at the clock on the mantle as if he was timing her.

When he broke his silence, he could have been any stranger on the street. "Can't be helped, Huffy. We just have to take it as it comes."

What was left other than groveling on the floor to beg forgiveness. She wasn't interested in being any man's doormat, perhaps he was right in severing all feelings between them. "I meant what I just said, Turk."

"Let's get to serious talk, here."

"You're a cold devil."

"I don't intend to be killed by some Middle Eastern malcontent al quaeda that doesn't like the way I part my hair. I fought those bastards for six years and they still don't like me. Or my country."

His true personality slipped out easily enough. The way he would talk to eight brothers all competing to be top dog. "May I go now?"

"Help yourself." He swept his arm out in a courtly manner, the action insulting after his crude remarks.

"You're too kind."

She hadn't gotten out into the hall before she heard the liquor bottle clinking against a glass. Turk wasn't a drunk. Something else was eating at him.

She paused, wishing they were making love, not being caught up in the ugliness of the outside world.

"Huffy."

The sound of his voice touched her emotions like soft snow in the moonlight. Could she trust herself to answer like an adult?

"What is it?" She looked over her shoulder to see if he followed her. He hadn't.

"Sorry. It was nothing." His words were a bit muffled, coming from his office. "Dinner will be late tonight."

Dinner? What did she care about dinner? She probably would never regain her appetite after this.

Get yourself busy. Get out of his sight and he won't hurt your incredibly silly feelings.

Hugging her arms around herself, Abigail hurried to the great room. Shane lolled on a sofa, watching something he called NASCAR. "Shane. Are you scared?"

He flicked his hand negligently, and grinned at her. "Can't run all your life. I trust Turk to keep us alive."

She sat beside him, welcoming the arm he lay over her shoulders. "I wish I was as confident. He hates me for showing up here on his doorstep, dragging all kinds of trouble with me. I've really messed up."

Just like old times, her whining and Shane babying her. He popped a snack cracker into his mouth before changing the channel to a movie.

"I know pretty chicks like you don't dig cars." He offered her a chunk of cheese. "Don't worry so much. We'll get out of this and you can pick up where you left off."

Was he telling her he was going his own way if they beat the odds?

"Did Turk say anything about--later?"

"Didn't have to. He's crazy for you, babe."

New fear weighed down around her. This could all go so wrong, the loss too horrible to think about. Abigail leaned against her longtime friend and thought about her choices. They were few, but critically important to the rest of her life.

Turk didn't seem to have any problem telling her to move along. He'd swept her from his thoughts and gone back to treating her with cool distaste. He was breaking her heart.

* * * *

Turk managed to get out of the house unseen, leaving his houseguests watching the boob tube. He concealed himself behind several large lilac bushes, punching in Gun's phone number.

"Yeah, Gun. It's me."

"Trouble already got there?" Gun's concern reverberated in his voice.

"Not yet, but if he does what I expect, he's not driving in from Santa Fe."

"He'll be flying, I expect." The short silence was punctuated by the neigh from the stables. "Soon as I grab Ram and a chopper, we're heading your way. Be there before dawn."

Turk's body relaxed. "It's not like I can't handle this freak. Man, I have Huffy here." He scrubbed his hand over his face. "This is going to be a lot harder with her being a prime target."

"Turk, I know we don't normally involve local law enforcement on our jobs, but maybe this time it's justified."

Looking at the back door of the house, Turk shook his head. "No. I have all the ammo I need and everyone knows what to expect. We'll handle the situation."

"Okay, my brother. We're on our way."

"I'm not going anywhere."

"Vaya con Dios."

"Y tu, hermano."

Turk didn't like the deep silence falling around the lodge. Too early for the crushing quiet of deep night time.

Maybe he should take a walk, just to be sure nothing was out of place. *Damn.* He'd been so sure of himself when he came home from the sandbox. All it took to rattle his nerves was a sweet smelling woman with the devil in her blue eyes.

What the hell was that? His nerves stretched tight, ready to snap like that twig he'd heard in the ancient cherry orchard.

Ten yards away, a small buck scampered across the yard, on his way to the woods behind the lodge. That could be perfectly natural, but on the other hand, something may have spooked him.

Turk hunkered down, waiting to see if anything followed the deer. Five minutes later, nothing happened to keep him out in the deepening chill.

He kept the Glock in hand until he was back in the house with the door was locked. As an extra safety measure, he dropped the security bar into place across the door.

She came into the kitchen, staring at the weapon in his hand.

"Nothing wrong, Huffy." He placed the weapon on the counter. "I'm going to make some barbeque sandwiches if that's okay for supper."

Her tiny shrug told him she had no opinion on the subject. "That's fine." She went to the dish cabinet and took down plates and glasses. It looked good on her, the homemaker stuff. "Is it too late for coffee?"

"Never too late for a cup of Joe." *Why was it, whenever you were trying your damndest to avoid touching a woman, you seemed to be all over them? Accidentally brushing their arm, bumping into their ass?*

She looked up with a modest smile the last time he inadvertently pressed his arm against her breasts while getting napkins from the shelf.

This was a good time to ask her what she wanted to do as soon as this drama was finished. God, he wanted to know.

"Huffy."

"Yes." She turned her glorious blue gaze on him, and he wanted to grab her up in his arms to kiss her forever.

"It can wait."

Coward.

"Turk."

He spun like a top to look at her. "Yeah?"

"Where do I sleep tonight?"

Aw, shit.

"That's up to you, Huffy. Move Shane into one of the other eight rooms."

You damn fool. Look at the face of the woman you hurt so often. She may not want forever, but Lord, she needed him tonight.

"I meant, is there space for me in your room?"

"I'll make room."

An hour later, Turk began to lose patience, and balls for the things he had to say top Huffy.

Where was she? Turk had showered, and hit the sack, grabbing that corny book he'd found and pretended to read whenever he thought Huffy was joining him.

She was still in the kitchen helping Shane. *Damn.* They'd had enough time to fix a Thanksgiving dinner.

Earlier, passing by the kitchen, he couldn't believe he was hearing the whirr of the blender followed by the smell of coffee brewing. Turk figured together they should be able to destroy every small appliance he owned.

Was she ever coming to bed? Finally, she'd said goodnight to Shane and padded into the bedroom.

The noise didn't disturb him. To the contrary. Her brushing her teeth sounded down right musical. The water ran, then that funny looking facial scrub thing hummed into action.

Turk moved higher on his stack of pillows to listen. *Plink, plink,* then lids closing on her mysterious creams and lotions. At last, the light was snuffed.

Eyeing her over the book, he grinned. She'd missed getting a big hunk of hair in her headband, and it flopped like a birds tail at the back of her head. He went back to scanning the words on the dog-eared page.

No use. He couldn't be anywhere but here with her.

It all seemed so damn natural, him closing the book, tossing it onto the nightstand. Huffy dropping her robe on the floor. How calm he must look to her, moving over when she turned the quilt down.

If his nerves tensed any more, he'd catapult from the bed. Would she hear it in his voice?

"Ready for the light to go out?"

She made that soft little sighing sound that belonged only to her. "Um-hm."

"Goodnight, Huffy."

Is that the best you can come up with? No wonder she thinks you're no more than a dumb cowboy.

He inhaled with complete relaxation, letting the glow of happiness seep into his hide. This felt so right, like it had always been him and Huffy. Then why was he so scared of this situation?

After several minutes of sheet rustling, pillow punching and changing the quilt to the foot of the bed, she did what he longed for, and yet, dreaded. She touched him.

Her slender arm claimed him completely, resting light over his waist, taking his soul. *Please, baby. Roll over. Turn your back to me.*

He tensed with the force of a real war screaming through his body, torrid passion that raced through his blood threatened to become a major explosion. Dumbest thing he ever tried, hiding a major erection from a woman. *Hell, play it right and she'll never know.*

"Turk, hold me."

How was he to fight with this, the scent of her perfume, invading his senses with its delicate tendrils of seduction?

He wasn't made of wood. "How close?"

Chapter 21

Waves of sweet relief washed away Abigail's fear and hesitancy to go to his room.

She answered his question with open honesty and desire to tell him her heart beat only for him.

"Until I can't take it anymore." Abigail went into his arms and pressed her shivering body to his.

Was he thinking of her, wondering about how she might stay with him for the rest of her life? Of course not. He's a normal man and they don't plan their lives around women who tear off their clothes and have sex in the kitchen. The bare truth hurt, sent her seeking his warmth, anything to be closer to him.

"Huffy, you're too much for my heart, you know." His soft drawling words confused her.

He had no idea how frightened and confused she was. Turk was the first complete man she'd known, the first to put a burning need in her heart to stay with him.

But, that wasn't what he wanted to know. *Bite your tongue. Don't say something whiny and clingy.*

He gazed at her, waiting. "Did you hear me?" he asked a bit more loudly.

"I heard you." He gently traced the curve of her jaw. Abigail couldn't be quiet. "I don't know what you mean."

"I'm thirty-five."

In the dim light filtering down from the autumn moon, his strong profile was visible. Another rhyme? What was he getting at? Age?

"If you're saying you are too old for me, that isn't true." To cover her ignorance of not knowing if he'd meant something else, she quickly added, "of course age is a matter of one's outlook on life."

"Bull." He lifted up to rest on his elbow. "You know that isn't what I meant. I don't have much to offer a woman like you, Huffy."

This was his brand of warning, ominous like the cold sound of rain on the window pane.

"You don't have room in your heart for me, just your bed?" She clung to his waist, lifting her head to see him more clearly.

His hands gripped her shoulders and he pulled her against him, drawing in a rough breath. "I'm trying to tell you, that after this is over, you have to catch that flight to Mexico. No one will stop you."

So, this was it, the end before it really started? *Don't get sloppy and cry, or blubber that you'll die without him. Even though it's true.*

"I have no say?"

"No. You don't."

"You're telling me you want me to leave?"

"I'm telling you to go find what you were after before landing here."

She was grateful the darkness hid her terrible pain. What had she expected? Her knight in shining spurs and a beat up Stetson? She'd asked for it, lowering her guard and tossing sensibility aside.

Okay, you've just been told to find a new life by the man you'll never get over. If only she could breath and make this exit look good.

She threw off the sheet and left his bed, scrambling in the dark for her robe.

Turk sat up to grumble at her. "Where you going?"

"My room's upstairs."

"Shane's in your room."

"I know that. Go back to sleep."

"I never was asleep!" His loud groan echoed around the room. "Stop talking nonsense. I can't sleep while some nut case is making plans to kill us all." He exhaled in apparent exasperation. "Come back to bed and let me keep you safe."

"No."

How useless did she look to him? Where had her common sense flown to? *You know very well where it went, Abigail. You lost everything to him and you'll never regain it. Get out of here while you can. He's already given you the heave-ho.*

She turned the brass knob, but Turk's hand stopped her from opening the door. That's what she wanted, wasn't it? Any excuse to be back in his arms.

"I'm sorry about that crap, Huffy." He caught the belt of her robe in his fingers, slowly pulling her to him. "I meant for that to come out different. Not hurt you."

"I can't sleep with you anymore, Turk."

"I said I was sorry. No use both of us not getting any sleep."

"That isn't enough." Keeping tears from spilling took every last shred of pride. "And you'll never know what is enough until one morning you wake up and need me, and I'll be gone."

She hated him and loved him as he picked her up and kissed her hard. "Lady, I'd find you if it meant flying through ten constellations and behind the moon."

He didn't take her to bed, but set her down to pull her close, his intake of breath cooling a little of her hurt ego. *Oh, its okay, shiver if you must.* His hand cuddling her breast was better than any apology he could ever think up.

His voice was rough with desire. "Are you getting bigger?"

The observation pleased her, and was true. She did swell with her passion.

She heard her own laugh as it drifted in the darkened room like a sultry web. "You've grown some too, cowboy."

Oh, yes, he wanted her, the proof was in his quickened breathing and his erection straining against her belly.

He turned her, pressed her back to the wall, then lifted her to ride his thigh. "I need you, baby."

He needs you tonight, but what about tomorrow?

I don't care about tomorrow. Just tonight.

A firestorm swept over Abigail, carrying her to new and dangerous places too near the sun, flinging her into an inferno with no escape.

"Abigail." His impassioned way of saying her name stroked her libido, whetting the ache to be one with him.

"My darling."

No stopping the tide of fire now. Not while his mouth covered her nipple and firm lips sucked hard to drive her wild. He moved on to doing a man's business between her legs, dipping his talented fingers into her heat, stroking and squeezing her sensitized clit.

This was as far as she'd ever gone, on a wild flight riding a fireball of a man's leg, and coaxing him to give her more, more shocking hot joy from his fingertips.

"Damn, Huffy." His whisper was hoarse and urgent against her lips. "I meant to go down on you, but I can't wait this time."

"I'll wait. Just hurry now."

Beyond ready, she had no control over her body, groaning while bucking her hips against his thigh until she cried out in ecstasy.

His cock was hot as sin in her hand, heavy and pulsing. Everything was perfect when he lifted her, opening her for his penetration with excruciating slowness.

Exquisite! She tightened around the pressure of his member, tilting her head back in luxuriant joy.

Had that been thunder? No. Too close and damn it, just outside the bedroom door! The clatter ripped into her senses again, the noise that threatened her secret world of man and woman feeling nothing but carnal pleasure.

It wouldn't stop! In a daze, she heard Turk curse, his shuddering breath reminding her of where they were.

"What the hell?" Turk pulled from her and grabbed his sweat pants before running from the bedroom to the office door. She caught the glint of the weapon he'd laid on the desk.

"Turk!" She fell on the floor, scrambling for her robe. "Wait. Don't leave me!"

"Turk." That was Shane, sounding as afraid as she was. "There's someone in my closet!"

He opened the door to reveal Shane shaking like a leaf, hair standing on end and face white as a ghost. "Get in here, damn it."

Abigail clutched her robe about herself, clinching her hands to control their trembling, amazed anyone had gotten past Turk. "Do I need my gun yet?"

Turk looked over his shoulder at her, shook his head and motioned for her to stay put. "I'm going to see what's going on." He pointed to Shane.

"Grab that rifle from over the fireplace and take care of Huffy. Guard the door."

Turk shut the door to his office, grimacing with unleashed testosterone. His legs were near collapse from the tension of putting Huffy against the wall. *Damn it.*

Upstairs, the door to Huffy's room yawned open. He stepped inside the room, her scent of sweet Persian Lilac replaced with the shaving balm Shane had borrowed.

Turk wanted to be pissed off at the kid for ruining what could have been the best sex of his life, but that was thinking stupid. It was his fault for once again plowing through the rules. Everything was on hold until the Arab was stone cold.

Aggravated to the point of anger, Turk stood looking around, ready to leave until a familiar sound jerked him back to the moment.

Meow.

He turned on the table lamp, the soft glow revealing Lucy where she blinked at him from the open closet door.

"Damn it, Lucy. You've had those kittens in there, haven't you?"

She'd obviously spurned the nice nursery he'd provided for the perfumed jungle of Huffy's closet.

With all the junk piled in the closet, it wasn't easy for him to see what was happening. In the furthest corner, in a nest made of something pink and probably expensive, two gray-striped kittens squirmed and complained with amazing volume.

Turk exhaled roughly, rocking back on his heels in quiet reflection, glad as hell the commotion had been Lucy and her babies.

"Lord. I'll bet they're girls too." He backed out of the closet, already wondering what he was to do with them. He took a final parting shot at his feline guest. "Congratulations. I should have named you Hooker."

He switched off the small lamp and started down the stairs, stopping to look out the widow overlooking the deserted front yard. Nothing but a few leaves hurrying ahead of the cold wind.

Cold was something he'd almost forgotten the sensation of while in the Middle East, the cold clean scent of ass deep snow. Biting cold, drive you to bed cold, and he'd missed it. Two things he never wanted to see again, Camels and rubble.

A shudder hit him unexpectedly, and he closed his eyes against the vague fear squeezing his gut. "Suck it up, Gunnison. You can handle this."

Chapter 22

Abigail pressed her ear to the door, listening for Turk's footsteps. "He's been gone so long." She'd wanted to tag after him, but Shane stopped her. "He must be in trouble."

"You're not serious?" Shane held the huge rifle with surprising confidence. "Turk's never met any trouble he couldn't handle." He lowered his voice. "Until he met you."

His meaning was clear. He liked Turk's rough ways and had taken on many of his mannerisms. Shane always emulated his heroes. This one would be harder than the rest.

Right now, she couldn't be bothered with his assessment of her personality. She was anxious about Turk's welfare.

The quiet of the office was split by a familiar voice from the hall.

"Okay. You can open up now."

"Are you Turk?"

The silence following Shane's try at humor lasted several seconds.

"Open the door. Now."

Abigail laughed with nervous relief, her fear melting with the moment of levity. Even Turk gave her a quick smile when he came through the door.

"What was it?" She kept her hands busy, re-tying the belt of her robe.

"Kittens." Turk glanced at the mantel clock as it chimed two a.m.

"I want to see them." He stopped her in mid-stride.

"Maybe we should wait until morning. Lucy wasn't too happy about me being up there."

Abigail bit back her disappointment. "Okay, tomorrow then."

"You two catch some shut-eye." Turk checked the lock of the front door for the tenth time.

Shane covered a yawn. "Suits me. I'm a light sleeper, so just yell when the stuff hits the fan." He didn't see Turk's tight smile, headed back upstairs, leaving them alone.

"I'm staying with you. I'm not going to scream and get in your way."

The ticking of the clock seemed uncommonly loud. What was he thinking? At last, he hooked his arm over her shoulders.

"I know you won't." He gazed at her, question in his eyes. "So, when did you start thinking that you were in my way?"

Should she tell him the truth, that she'd been in everyone's way from the day she was born? She chose to slide over that gem in her biography.

"Oh, come on, Turk." The smile on her lips quivered dangerously close to being replaced by a sobbing scowl. "You know it's true. But, what I said. I meant. I'll shoot that gun and not hide."

He wrapped his arms around her, the fact that frightening gun was still in his hand didn't bother her.

"Huffy, we need to talk. A lot." He led her to the hearth room and sat her down on the oversized leather sofa. "Want to talk about when you were a kid?" He laughed softly, hugging her to his side. "You got a couple of years to hear about mine?"

He was so confident in his big old family, unafraid to talk about mothers, fathers and brothers. Family. She had nothing to compare to that.

"Sure, go ahead." She leaned her head back to watch his face as he talked. "I'd love to hear all of it."

There was that unnamed look of pride and pleasure on his face that she'd seen on lots of other people, pride and love for family.

"I came late, number eight of nine boys." He relaxed against the cushions and smiled at her. "Yep, it all began on a ranch outside Dallas, held together by a father as strong as Atlas and smart as Einstein."

"Your mother?" Abigail was deeply interested in the woman that he called momma.

"Beautiful, patient, loving, and knew how to use a switch." His voice softened. "If she hadn't held us down, I don't know where we would have ended up."

So Turk was a bad seed, probably a lot like her. No wonder she was crazy for him. Kindred souls. "What did you do that was so bad? Why did you stop?"

"Who said I stopped?" He kissed her forehead and went on. "I didn't steal or hot-wire cars, even though Gun taught me how. He was my biggest problem. His dares were too hard to pass up. Fight this guy and I'll give you my new rifle. Ask that girl for a...to have a good time and I'll give you money to do it on."

Was that what brothers did? The men in her life had never shared their feelings about family. "I saw the picture in the great-room. The other men, they are your brothers? All military?"

"That's them. Gun is hardcore Ranger Delta Force in the family. Ram is Navy, a highly decorated Seal. The ladies man, as we call him. Can't keep a girl more than time for shore leave to end."

"The other one, he seemed very young."

"Yeah, that's the baby in the bunch. Diego. We call him Shooter."

Hearing about his family was far more than she'd ever expected. What was she to tell him if he insisted on knowing her secrets? She simply wouldn't reveal them.

"Cookie seemed to think there were fights in your home." Oh, Lord, had she said something wrong? He exhaled and sat up.

"There were, but nothing serious."

"Over girls, I suppose." Her attempt at humor gutter-balled.

"Sometimes."

She couldn't help it, she had to know. "You lost a girl to one of them?"

"Ram and Gun kept a running bet on taking my girls. It didn't matter. Just a game."

Abigail was disgusted by her delight that Turk hadn't been in a real relationship. She covered her glee with concern. "I didn't mean to pry."

"Forget that. We have something to take care of right now. He laughed and stood, pulling her up.

What was wrong with her? Scared of his past and yet dying to know? Please don't let him ask me anything. I don't want to seem small in his eyes. Change the subject.

"Where are we going?" She hoped to bed.

"To pick out your weapon. Then you're going to catch a few winks."

They returned to the office where he removed the Navajo rug that covered an old leather bound trunk. He opened the cedar-lined chest, and brought out a quilt made of tiny squares of prairie flowers and butterflies.

"How beautiful." Abigail touched the quilt, marveling at the many delicate stitches.

"My great grandmother, Cecilia Montoya Perez Gunnison left this to grandson number eight." He grinned. "I won that lottery."

He went to the gun case and opened it. The moment of reckoning had come. Chose your weapon. Words she'd never thought to hear. Yet, here she stood, checking out the selection, pointing to the ones she thought fit her hand, only to have him shake his head. Finally, he picked one.

"I can't work that!"

"Sure you can."

"It's huge."

"Open your hands. Hold them out, palms up."

She licked her dry lips. "It's too heavy."

"How do you know? Here."

She lifted the weight of the smooth wood and steel in her hands and smiled. "I can hold it."

He caught her arm when she tried to sight the weapon. "Don't need to do that. This twelve-gauge, double barrel has a scatter wide enough to take out a platoon." He pressed her hand down to rest the stock on her hip. "Don't aim. From there, you just pull trigger. Take your finger off the trigger, please."

Just shoot from the hip. She was capable of that. "I'm ready. You can depend on me."

"I never doubted it." He took the rifle, and nodded toward the couch. "Lie down. I'll take this watch."

Bless him. Her eyes were drooping in spite of all that was going on. "Maybe for just a few minutes."

Oh, yes. This was heaven, cozy under a special quilt and her beautiful warrior watching over her. *Bilge water, Abigail. He's just doing what he knows to keep everyone alive. He's a good man that thinks it's his duty to protect idiots like you.*

He'd turned off all the lights, and moved around, checking windows and door-locks, coming back to reassure her things were okay.

In a single thudding heartbeat, a dark and forbidding change seemed to smother the room. Turk had left the office. She fought panic that leapt crazily in her heart.

Lord, if you must take someone, let it be me.

She got up and put on her slippers, taking up the weapon Turk had assigned her. Out in the hall, Turk glanced over his shoulder when she approached him.

"Come here." He held out his hand. "I've thought this over. I want you to hightail it down to the basement, and lock yourself in the supply room. If anyone opens that door, blow the hell out of them, one barrel at a time."

"It might be you."

"No, no. Won't be us."

"How long must I wait?"

"Till I call you on this cell phone." He dropped the phone he held into the pocket of her robe.

"Please, don't ask me to do that." Tears sprang hot and salty from her eyes to spill down her cheeks. She couldn't breathe, clutched uselessly at his shoulders.

"Got to be this way." He held her face in his hands to kiss her. "Go on now, honey. Listen for my call."

"Please, don't make me leave."

He clamped his lips over clenched teeth, not saying another word as he took her arm to hurry her down the short flight of stairs to the basement. He opened the supply room door and put her inside. His gaze didn't settle on hers until he handed her the rifle.

He touched the double lock on the door, silently reminding her to lock up after he left.

"I'm coming back for you, Huffy."

"Turk."

He was gone, leaving her to wait in terror of losing him.

Chapter 23

His heart pounded like a fifteen inch gun off the deck of the USS Sam Houston as he ran back to check the front of the house.

Sweat blinded him for a minute, burning like acid in his eyes. He could make split second decisions, but wasn't willing to make mistakes when Huffy's life hung in the balance.

Damn! Had he done the right thing? Uncertainty tore at his gut. What if the Kufu got by him, found her? Could she pull the trigger? He fought for control to stay where he was while instinct hammered his brain, telling him to go back for her.

He froze at a shuffling sound at the top of the stairs. His neck hair rose.

"Damn it, Shane." He mopped moisture from his face. "Sorry, man. That's nerves talking. You doing okay up there?"

"Hell, yeah." Shane's quiet reply intermingled with the rustle of paper and some bravado. "When's that sucker coming?"

Turk grinned at the irony of the situation. "He'll be here." He leaned against the door jam, curiosity getting the better of him. "What's that rattling I hear?"

"Abbey gave me a piece of cake wrapped in wax paper." A brief silence followed. "Want some?"

Turk didn't answer, a rush of adrenalin closed his throat and threatened to stop his heart. Outside, the horses were loose, running in a wild frenzy through the yard and around the house.

The grim reaper had come calling. Meet him with all you have, Gunnison.

"Turk!"

"Quiet."

An ominous sound, like distant thunder erupted. Terrified horses fought for escape from something in the corral and crashed wildly over the patio and onto the porch. Turk heard his property being destroyed in the onslaught, but only worried about the livestock.

Time to throw some light on what the hell was going on out there.

"Watch your head, Shane." With the flip of a switch, the scene outside looked like high noon in the glaring security lights.

Glancing down at his state of undress, Turk took off for the bedroom. He yanked on jeans and boots and a shirt he found on the floor. On the way out, he replenished his armory with a high-powered rifle and another forty-five, plenty of ammo and his hat.

By the time he got back to the door, most of the horses had taken off for safer pastures, leaving behind a lingering dust cloud. He snuffed the lights, leaving the yard in pitch darkness. Using night vision glasses, he searched desperately for any sign the freak had come closer to the house.

Turk held his breath, trying to pick out a human from the shadows and brush tumbling across the patio. He released the breath in a rush of cold worry. There was movement near the stables, then the unmistakable flare of orange and red lighting up the scene outside.

Fire. The bastard's set my stables on fire!

He glanced up at Shane where he hunkered down on the landing, looking steady as any buddy he'd fought with. "I'm going to put this fool to sleep before he burns the house down."

"Wait!" Shane started down the stairs. "I'll go with you."

"No. Remember Huffy! We can't leave her alone. Take care of her. Okay?"

The bravado froze in his veins as he recognized the thudding sounds of slugs grinding into the logs of the house.

Flames, orange and red shot skyward as hay and feed ignited. A hard jolt of foreboding rocked him.

The house. Kufu Rama Fa was here and intended to torch the house!

"Shane. Come down here."

Riding the handrail down, Shane looked more like a Gunnison than a brief acquaintance.

He stared with solemn eyes at Turk. "What's up?" The kid had lots of guts to go with his devil may care attitude. "Want me to lay down some fire?"

Turk looked around, choosing his exit to meet the devil. "I've changed my mind. Go get Huffy and keep her with you no matter what."

With a nod, Shane took off. Turk waited until he heard them on the stairs before going to the kitchen. If he saw Huffy, he wouldn't be able to leave her. Time to roll.

He chose a window where the limbs of an old apple tree hugged the panes protectively and hid him as he slipped into the darkness.

He wanted to run and find the bastard laying waste on his home, to choke the life from his body. But, he couldn't. Not yet.

Take your time, Gunnison. Ease back on the hammer.

Six or seven horses moved outside the corral, shying at something across the torn up yard.

Indecision ate at his gut. Had he done the right thing, leaving her with Shane? Too late to chew that over. He had one mission. Put down the mad dog.

A shadow fell ten feet tall over the walls of the tool shed. Kufu was openly moving around, daring Turk to show himself.

Kufu was the ultimate egomaniac, coming alone to wage war.

Turk called softly to his horse and the big stallion followed his voice, lowering his head to accept a calming touch from his master.

"Steady, boy." Turk crouched beside the horse and coaxed him forward. "Nice and steady."

Smoke billowed to be caught in the gusting wind, only to come back and wrap around him in a choking blanket. He covered his nose, turning to look back at the house. The place was still dark and in one piece.

A break came in the sound of someone coughing. The bastard was choking. Turk grinned with satisfaction, knowing Kufu was reaping some of his own evil reward. The sound spooked his horse and the animal reared before charging through the smoke, leaving him a sitting duck.

New realization cut through the hell going on around him. Gunfire from an automatic rifle ripped into the already mad scene.

You're the target, stupid. Run!

He cursed his legs that were heavy as lead as he tried to make a break for cover. Smoke burned his eyes and filled his lungs. Hot lead hummed past his head, forcing him to eat dirt, crawl like a worm toward the corral.

Through holes in the drifting smoke, he caught sight of the new tool shed. *Damn.* It too was in flames.

That meant the house was next.

Not while my heart beats.

Kufu was smart enough to keep moving, making himself less visible. He obviously moved around among the already frightened horses that raised hell, snorting and fighting for space.

The ground under Turk vibrated, and his senses coiled like strands of barbed wire around his chest. A full clip exploded over his head and set the herd into another wild run in his direction.

He was going to be dead if he didn't move fast.

Turk took a chance and rolled several times, coming to rest against the water pump near the stable. It saved his bacon while the horses plowed past him.

Steel shod hooves missed him by inches while he hugged the pump housing. Mayhem ruled, the noise of panicked animals deafening.

The powerful wave of horseflesh streamed on past, leaving behind clumps of torn up sod and shattered fencing.

Turk jumped to his feet, freezing to the spot hearing the chatter of the automatic laying out a line of fire on the house.

Rage squeezed Turk's gut. The reality that someone waged war on his home straightened out his problem of hesitation. He could no longer play it safe while the windows of his home were blasted out and the frames splintered like balsa wood.

Waiting was not an option.

His break came on the wind after it changed direction, tearing a big hole in the billowing smoke.

He strained his eyes to see, to be sure of his target. There he was, the devil wearing a familiar black pajama outfit he'd seen a thousand times in the Mid-east, busy firing two AR17's at the house. The fucking weasel.

Turk ran forward, shouting to get Fa's attention.

"Over here, sweetheart!"

What the hell was wrong with the freak? He barely glanced at him before firing at the house again instead of unloading on him.

In stunned slow motion, his question was answered. A crazy kaleidoscope of action whirled around before him, accompanied by the distant report of a much lighter weapon.

Shane! The kid was outside, coming like a commando through the wreckage. He squeezed off several rounds, drawing Kufu to him, jumping a pile of broken lawn chairs.

The next second, he was in the air, suspended for one full heartbeat, arms extended, head thrown back before pitching backwards.

The horror of the scene splintered Turk's mind. Dear God, that could be Abigail too. Self-preservation no longer mattered.

He primed the rifle as he walked, not taking his eyes off Kufu standing over Shane. He leveled his weapon on the downed kid, whipping around to look at Turk when he yelled.

"Here! Here I am, you son-of-a-bitch. Deal with me!"

The devil didn't cut down on Turk as he expected, instead, turned to finish off Shane.

The single shot Turk fired tore through Kufu's heart, ending the war. Turk fell to the ground to wait for the next round of ammo to come his way. It didn't happen. The dead man had indeed come alone.

Kufu lay crumpled in a tattered, dark heap, mindless of the hoofs trampling him as the rest of the herd stampeded off into the woods, miraculously avoiding Shane.

* * * *

Abigail stopped breathing after finding Turk had left the house.

How could he leave her to wonder if he was wounded, or worse? She had to be where he was. Shane took off to help Turk, leaving her to make her own decisions. She had to find her beloved.

Gripping the rifle in one hand, Abigail pressed her palms to the wall, using it as a guide in the smoky darkness to find the door.

Flaring light came through the splintered door that hung crazily on its frame.

She remembered her brief conversation with Shane before he took off.

"I'm coming with you."

"No. You're not. He said you stayed put."

"Shane!"

Then he was gone. She refused to stand around not knowing what had happened to Turk. Scrambling to catch up with Shane proved impossible. Smoke and noise confused her, leaving her with no sense of direction.

What was that? Shane yelling at someone. Maybe at Turk. Her lips curved up in a smile of relief. No, that was Turk. He was angry, threatening someone. Kufu!

More gunfire, then a span of silence. She ran toward the sound, falling on her face in her hurry. There was more gunfire, a thunderous crash and an agonizing silence before Turk's strong voice split the silence.

She screamed after another roaring explosion came from a nearby gun. She could barely make out the identity of the shooter.

"Turk!" Through the smoke, she saw him kneeling on the ground, talking desperately on someone. He swiped his forehead with his sleeve and leaned down. She heard his beseeching words.

"Shane! Come on, son. Breathe."

She gave a strangled cry, running to throw her arms around Turk, but was brought up short by what she saw.

"Come here," Turk yelled at her. "Take over while I get a blanket. Hurry, Abigail."

"But, he's bleeding…I can't stop it!"

Turk grabbed her arm, pulling her to her knees. "Press down hard and don't let up on the pressure."

"He's dying. Do something."

"No he's not. I've called for help." He took a step, ready to bolt away.

"Turk, stay here, please."

"Damn it, Abigail. Just do it!" he looked angry and a deep scowl on his face.

She went into wracking sobs after Turk's strong response. She was useless, and the truth cut like a sword through her heart.

Abigail had never seen blood in such great proportion or a face as ashen as Shane's. He groaned, the sound barely audible.

"Shane." She leaned down to speak to him, her hair falling into his chest. No words could describe the depth of her devastation, no amount of tears would erase what had happened. "This is my fault. All my fault. Please look at me."

The sudden slash of light over the yard blinded her. Fear squeezed her heart, making her positive she would faint. The killer was back! She grabbed the forty-five Shane had dropped.

A car of some type, roared up the drive and spun a wide circle in front of the house, spraying gravel against the broken fencing. Powerful headlights cut through the smoke, leaving particles of dust to dance crazily in the air.

Two men jumped from out of the truck, both carrying weapons.

"Turk!" She screamed his name and hoisted the pistol to stop the strangers. The hair trigger of the pistol clicked into action, the shot exploding before she could take good aim.

"Hey." One of them yelled at her and the two men quickly separated to avoid being shot. "Turk, get out here and take hold of your woman!"

Oh God. These had to be Turk's brothers. Brash and loud.

She dropped the weapon and cried out. "Here. Please help us. He's dying."

The one that had yelled, ran toward her, holstering his weapon.

"Move over honey. I'll take care of him." He knelt beside her, staring at Shane for a split second. "Who's this kid?"

"Shane." Her voice shook with tension and she briefly resisted him taking her hand away from Shane's chest.

"Where's Turk?" He yelled to the man that had been with him. "Find him."

Chapter 24

Turk recognized his brother's voices. He instantly began to breathe easier.

"Gun," he answered, running from the house with blankets and towels. "Thank God you're here."

Ram, the quieter, more thoughtful of them all, grabbed him in a bear hug, planting a kiss on his cheek.

"Sorry we weren't here to help."

"You're here. That's all that matters."

Abigail, his Abigail stared at him with wide, tear-filled eyes. She appeared unable to comprehend the devastation around her. Still keeping watch over Shane as Gun worked on him.

Turk blamed himself for the carnage around him , most of all the horrific trial the fragile beauty in her blood soaked robe and hair burnished red with the same blood had seen.

If he'd been better prepared, put his pride aside and called the local law, maybe this wouldn't have happened.

Hadn't he promised that nothing would harm her again? Abigail had no reason to trust him, or any other man who'd entered her life. His heart plummeted in disgust.

On the ground lay a kid with little chance of making it. His joy for life had always glinted in his eyes and the smart-assed way he talked foretold nothing like this would be in his future. The towel bandages and blankets for the shock was the best they could do for him. God willing, it would be enough.

Turk looked up, his nerves tightening like springs. "Where's that chopper?" He helped Abigail to her feet, hugging her close, trying to comfort her. Her words stunned him.

"If Shane dies, its because of me. He tried to help me and he's paying with his life." She was inconsolable, trying to touch Shane. "It should have been me."

Gun turned away to talk to Ram. They moved off to set out flares for the chopper to use when it set down.

This was too violent for any woman to be part of. Turk almost wished he was back in the sandbox where violence was everyday fare. It didn't fit here.

"Yo, Turk." Down the drive, Gun aimed the beam of his flashlight into the sky, letting him know the chopper was close.

Hearing the distinct *whup-whup* sound of rotor blades, his legs tensed in preparation to help load Shane into the aircraft.

Like something out of a nightmare, the small helicopter seemed to hover timelessly above the open field near his driveway, its heavy-duty lights cutting in and out of the smoke and dust filled sky.

Too many times overseas he'd done this same thing, loading boys inside a tin crate headed for the safety of a med-vac hospital for some fresh blood and maybe a real night's sleep, even if it was drug induced.

He'd been gripping Huffy's hand, memories tearing him apart. How could this have happened? Was there nowhere to hide from the devil?

"I have to help them. You stay here."

He trusted Ram to look after her. Ram was the one with the calming ways and was absolutely trustworthy, just like now, taking off his jacket to wrap around her. He didn't interfere with her steady sobbing, not trying to reassure her. He simply offered a strong arm and shoulder to lean on.

Turk wanted to cry, too, when he got a good look at Shane's face. Rice white, thin and frail. *God damn it!*

The EMT took all the information he could offer. It hadn't been much. He got their reassurance that Shane stood a good chance because of his youth and the quick first aid given him.

Before they lifted off, they hollered the name of the hospital Shane was being flown to. He wanted to get there as soon as possible.

Gun fell in beside him and they headed for the house. "The law will be here any minute. Got anything you want kept under wraps?"

"I say we call the FBI and turn it over to them." Turk wiped soot from his face. "I don't want Huffy messed with. Not now, not ever."

"Got it." Gun touched Turk's arm to slow him up. "I got some news before I left Dallas. Might make her a little happier."

"Spill it. She needs some good news."

"Seems her grandfather's had a change of heart." Gun shook his head. "He pulled his warrants to haul her back to Phoenix."

"About damn time." Turk grimaced. He couldn't wait to tell her the bit of good news.

"Wait. I'll need your help getting the boy out of the fire." Gun took out a small note pad and pen. "Okay, what did he tell you about the stiff over there? What was their relationship? Did he intend to do harm to the citizens of the United States?"

"Aw, hell. You know better." Turk pushed his brother's notepad aside. "He was trying to make some quick cash, didn't know that bastard was an enemy of the country. The kid only knows good haircuts and rock bands. Work it out, Gun. He's not being sent up the river over just being hired to run errands for Kufu. I'm not going to let it happen."

Backing off a step, Gun held up his hands in mock defense. "Good enough. I can make the whole thing go away." He stuffed the small spiral into his jacket pocket. "You like Ms. Huffington—a lot."

"What kind of dumb son-of-a-bitch statement is that?"

"Yeah, you're crazy about her."

"As easy as that to figure out, huh?" Turk shrugged, his gaze going to where Huffy stood. "Man, I'm glad you showed up. It was getting hairy."

"That's what the brothers Gunnison do." Together, they ran toward the house, Gun offering a morsel of his humor. "Lets go see how much damage Ram has done to your reputation."

Seconds later, they were forced into the ditch at the side of the road as a small convoy of trucks and cars raced past them.

Damn, couldn't they wait a few minutes? Turk's disgust was for the coroner and the bored Sheriff blazing a wide trail to the ranch.

Piling out of the huge RUV were the Sheriff and a deputy, hauling out shotguns and dogs. The dangerous looking fish pole antenna flopping back and forth on the back of the RUV completed the grade B movie scene.

"What the hell's that?" Nothing escaped Gun's eyes.

Turk shook his head. "He never got over the fade out of CB's. Likes the way it looks I guess."

"I'll take care of John Wayne, there. Gun glanced around. "Hell of a mess." He gestured to the Sheriff's car. "If the questions get too personal, I'll come get you." He lit one of his cigars he hadn't been able to give up. "I think Abigail needs you right now."

* * * *

Abigail put her hand in Turk's, too stunned to pay much attention to red lights or the wailing siren from the local authorities cars barreling down the lane toward the house.

She'd stopped crying when the helicopter lifted off. The moment it was out of sight, Turk steered her toward the house.

"We'll clean up and head for the hospital." He helped her step around the backdoor now scattered in pieces on the patio. "We'll be there by the time they know Shane's condition."

She wiped the robe's dirty sleeve over her eyes and nodded. "Okay. He'll be wondering where we are."

She couldn't recall the shower she'd taken or what Turk's brother had said as they drove away from the ranch.

Turk had practically dressed her in the cream slacks and white knit pullover she wore.

She smiled ruefully, touching her breast upon realizing she didn't wear a bra or panties.

Only a man truly in love would have thought she didn't need those cumbersome things. No, just a man doing the best he could for two uninvited people wrecking his life.

Worry about Shane weighed heavy as a boulder on her heart, fear over Turk's feelings for her also loomed in the background. She was sick with worry. The absolute certainty her life was heading for a painful lonely road relentlessly crushed her heart.

Turk glanced her way, her sigh louder than she'd expected.

"You going to be all right, Huffy?"

"Yes, fine." Her voice wavered a bit, yet she kept her tears dammed up.

The way he looked away so quickly told her he was concerned, not in love.

He took a cigar from the console. "You mind?"

"Not at all." Damn it. Could she sound any more like a crusty prig?

He smoked his cigar, looking calmer and far away in his thoughts. She wished there was a way to erase parts of her life.

From the first, she'd been too smitten with him to read the signals. She was too fast, too free with her love for a steady man like him. She was everything except his perceived idea on what a woman should be. There was no way to make him believe differently after getting dozens of faxes just brimming with half-truths and outright lies. Everything in them fortified his beliefs about her.

What was she thinking? The trollop way she'd had sex with him was the seal that doomed any chance she'd had with him. Fate had brought her to him, and she'd blown it.

That was just another added to the long list trailing behind her. She began to regain confidence, but didn't know where to begin. She wanted to explain, at least in part, why she did the things she did. Maybe that would wipe out al the reasons he had to not let himself fall in love with her.

Could she do it? If he loved her at all, she would be with him for the rest of her days. If not, she would survive.

Gather in your emotions, and tie them carefully. Even if he rejects you, don't make a scene.

Abigail closed her eyes, hoping she hadn't made too many mistakes or waited too long.

Conversation of any type stopped until they drove into the underground garage of the hospital.

Abigail pushed aside the problems that mattered only to her. Shane needed her full support now.

Turk led her to the admissions desk of the emergency room, taking on full responsibility in obtaining information. She loved him for that, for knowing she could never handle this alone.

"The surgery waiting room is just down the hall." He held her hand until they found a small sofa to sit on.

From habit, she leaned against Turk, hating her weak voice when she spoke. Her words would make all the difference in her future. "I have to tell you something, Turk."

"I think you need to hear this first." He glanced around the cluttered waiting room before continuing. "You don't have to be concerned about your grandfather giving you any more trouble. He's no longer going to try to force you back Phoenix."

That was it? No reassurance or excitement at looking forward to her being free to do as she pleased, free to stay with him with no fear of being found and humiliated?

He truly didn't want her. *Say something clever now, fool. He's waiting for you to say you'll be moving on. Oh, God.* She wanted to cry out for her mother, like she had so many times in the secrecy of her room.

Okay, Abigail. You've lost men before. Of course, he's the one you want. Stop crying and don't let him think he's ever going to forget you.

She chose the noble high road, and a casual acceptance of the situation.

"Then, that leaves me free to travel with no worry." Her lids burned, tears too close to hide. "I'll call my grandmother for airfare immediately."

"No need. I'll handle that."

Quick and clean. He'd just cut out and handed her foolish heart to her.

"That's so thoughtful, but I'd rather not put you out. My grandmother would rather I didn't depend on the kindness of strangers."

He smiled at her then, a sweet smile that reached his wonderful eyes, one she'd remember the rest of her life. His goodbye smile.

Chapter 25

Four hours late, the cramped waiting room became even more crowded with weary parents and their bored, hungry children. Abigail didn't care if she never heard the ring tone of a phone again.

A low widow-sill a short distance from the waiting room offered some relief where they drank their tenth cup of coffee and waited.

She tried to be positive, but as gurneys of pasty-faced patients were wheeled past them, her confidence sagged.

As if he read her thoughts, Turk took her hand. "Let's walk."

Grateful to be moving, Abigail walked beside him, hating herself for the selfish desires that crept into her heart, pushing aside her thoughts of poor Shane.

Turk touched her arm, stopping her. "The surgeon's coming this way."

Positive her knees would buckle, she held onto his arm for support. She read the doctor's expression as he strode swiftly toward them.

Impossible. He could have been thinking of his golf score. At last he made eye contact with her and held out his hand.

"You're with the Caloun boy?"

"His name is Shane." Turk sounded annoyed, his voice gruff. "What's going on?"

"He's remarkable actually. Young and strong and probably going to brag to his grandchildren about this."

Turk laughed aloud, and lifted her off her feet. Pure joy swept all the fear away, leaving her basking in relief.

The surgeon smiled indulgently, probably having seen this a thousand times. "His family has been notified. They are on their way." He glanced at his watch. "You won't be allowed to see him before morning. I recommend you go home and rest."

She didn't care if her voice shook as she spoke to the doctor. "Tell him we'll come back soon." She wanted to stop him from leaving, but he was already striding off down the hall. "What can we bring him?"

Calling back over his shoulder, the doctor assured her not to be too hasty. "No hurry. He'll be relying on the nurses to shave him and brush his teeth." His long green coat flared out behind him in his haste. "I must run now."

She grinned with elation, dabbing at her eyes. Turning her back to Turk saved her the trouble of explaining that she was being torn to pieces with conflicting emotions. Happiness for Shane. Torment for her loss.

Turk went to the water fountain and drank his fill. Abigail's thoughts turned to her departure from his life and ways of leaving lasting memories with him.

Look at him, so sure his life is on the straight and narrow once again. We'll see about that cowboy.

You'll never forget the strawberry preserves.

* * * *

That night, Abigail ate very little of the fried chicken Ram prepared for dinner. She drank coffee and listened to the men's conversation.

All were dark, copper hued and exuded the fire of strong family loyalty.

Turk took her eye frequently. He looked weary, the way he rubbed his neck said he needed rest.

This was Turk in his element, family and family secrets close to his heart. Ram grinned at her while Gun gave a lively account of fatherhood and passed around pictures of his family.

Turk attempted to pile more salad on her plate.

"No more, Turk."

"You've hardly eaten today."

He slid a plate next her coffee cup, a thick slice of pie on it. "I'll put ice cream on it if you like."

So sweet and ignorant of the facts. He broke her heart all over again.

Turk, I love you. Can't you see that?

She put her hand over her plate. "No, this is fine."

He freshened her coffee and leaned close to murmur in her ear. "You should be in bed."

Good Lord. Now what? His bed--her bed?

No. Not his bed. Speak up and save your self.

"You're right. I'll be going upstairs now." Her legs were like dry straw when she stood.

"You'll feel better down here." That was Ram again, thoughtful but so wrong. "We'll go upstairs and crash. Won't we Gun?"

"Oh hell yeah." Gun yawned a bit too hard and pushed away from the table. "We'll figure out the corral and stable tomorrow."

She took her plate to the sink. "Please, don't break up your conversation because of me." She placed her rinsed dishes in the dishwasher. "I'll just get my toothbrush from Turk's bathroom. Won't be but a minute."

Turk's expression didn't reveal much, but the grins exchanged between Ram and Gun spoke volumes on the fun they were having.

Tired of dancing around the situation, she opened the mystery door with a clanging announcement. "Gentlemen, just to put you at ease, Turk and I are no longer sleeping together."

Gun chuckled and Ram coughed. Turk groaned.

"Huffy. I'd feel better…"

She cut him off in mid sentence. "I'm sure of that." Covering a delicate yawn with her fingers, she smiled indulgently. "But, it wouldn't be fair to you."

"Jesus," he hissed under his breath.

Her ability to wrinkle his smooth exterior was a perk in their thorny relationship. "Goodnight all."

Three men sat as if glued to their chairs as she walked sedately from the room, a glow of pleasure warming her to the bone.

So, you're on the mend. You'll make that call and your new life begins.

* * * *

Turk didn't try to cover his anger after Abigail's smart-assed way of making her intentions known. How stupid of him to forget what a bitch she could be.

Across the room, Ram stood looking out the window, his thoughts obviously far from Lone horse. He hadn't commented on Huffy's colorful way of turning a phrase. If memory served Turk correctly, Ram probably still had feelings for a certain little blonde back in Dallas. The one that got away.

Gun took his coffee into the hearth room to make a call to the love of his life, Ali. The man had wound up with a woman far out of his league.

Groaning with the weight of being caught in a cyclone of emotion, Turk spread the insurance policy covering his property on the table.

The problem wasn't getting the structures rebuilt, but when. He had no idea how long he'd be tied up with trips to Denver and if Shane would need to come back to the lodge.

Aw hell, Gunnison. It's not that eating a hole in your gut. Being put out of the lady's bed is a hell of a lot more painful than you expected.

"You look like a man with problems." This couldn't be anything but harassment coming from Gun.

Turk glanced up and shrugged. "Did you decide to help me with this mess or what?"

"You know, Turk." Gun wore a smug expression. "We could stay in Denver if you need some privacy."

Turk's head snapped up. "What's this about?"

"Looks like we may have caused some tension between you and Abigail." Gun sipped his coffee and looked thoughtful. "She's okay, you know. Just the lady to settle you down."

The thought was way more appealing than Gun would ever guess. No need to let him know how close he'd come to the truth.

He snorted with derision. "Huffy isn't interested in settling me down."

Ram sat down beside him and peeled one of the apples Turk had brought home from Blue Bears.

"Now, mom's going to want to know all about Abigail." He had the balls to laugh.

Always the same, Ram never discussed his affairs, current or burnt out. Now, here he was, more than happy to add his two cents worth.

Turk folded the papers he'd been reading before reaching out to muss Ram's hair. "Aren't you the one carrying the torch for Miss Ice Panties of Dallas?"

Gun chuckled, the mischievous sound adding to the warmth of their inner circle. "I heard she was afraid of you, ran like a pack of wolves were after her at just the mention of the Gunnison name."

The male laughter reverberated around the room, temporarily banished Turk's heavy mood. He added fuel to Gun's assessment of his brother. "She ran from Gun and after Ram. She couldn't see the rest of us for his dust."

Ram stretched, combing his fingers through his hair. "We have an understanding now. It's her sister Shey that interests me." He groaned. "Trouble is, she gets that deer in the headlights look whenever I get so much as a block away from her."

"That girl!" Gun snorted with his judgment on the subject. "She's way too young for an old sea walrus like you."

"No shit." Turk visualized how he remembered the girl in question. "Does she still ride horses along the damn highway to scare the hell out of you?"

"She's grown up some." Ram's voice took on a gruff, cranky note. "She's been to college and is home now." He looked perturbed, jaw set and eyes narrowed. "Least, that's what I heard."

Turk and Gun grinned, calling off the teasing of their sibling.

The banter died down and Gun and Ram finally went upstairs to crash for the night.

Turk went to his room, taking a bottle of Jack with him. He stripped and crawled under the quilts, preparing to have a bedtime drink.

The TV reception sucked tonight and the soft, lingering smell of warm Persian lilac wouldn't let him drift off in the sleepy daze he desired.

He gazed up at the ceiling. Upstairs huffy probably slept in the splendor of her damned stubborn ways.

He rolled onto his side, hugging the pillow she'd favored.

Damn. Would she ever go to sleep?

Her footsteps were simple to follow overhead. To the closet. Then to the window. Next came the bathroom. At last silence.

Aw, shit. Now she was coming downstairs, apparently trying to be quiet. The creak on the old walnut steps gave her away.

Flinging the quilts aside, he pulled on his sweats and went to the office door to look out. No, it was none of his business what she was up to.

Well, it wouldn't hurt anything to check and see if she was okay. *Fool. Tell yourself anything just to see her.*

He opened the door, hesitating when he heard her clear voice. She was on the phone.

He was no eavesdropper and quietly closed the door. His gut felt as if he'd swallowed one of those wrecking balls.

Had he really been so secure and content a few weeks ago, or had he been living a fools dream?

This was no dream. When Huffy left him, there as no going back to the contented pasture bull feeling he'd once had.

He sat on the bed and punched his pillow.

If he ever clawed his way out of this pit, nothing would take him so far out of reality again. Pleasure like he'd known with Huffy was not meant to last, at least for a fool like him.

Chapter 26

Abigail had heard Turk's office door open last night. Her heart had leapt into her throat, hope that he'd speak to her a bubbling spring of need.

Much to her disappointment, he hadn't come to persuade her to give up the single life and make him the center of her universe. If only he knew that spot in her life was already taken by him.

She sighed, while folding a stack of her undergarments she'd taken from the dryer.

The house was quiet since the men had gone out, where she wasn't sure.

They'd discussed going to the sheriff's office and then to the lumber company. None of which interested her.

Turk had left the house with them and she hated to admit it, but she missed him terribly. For weeks, he'd filled her every moment with his larger than life persona. Now the realization that all was coming to an end hurt so badly she winced.

There was so little time before she'd have to leave the lodge and that meant never seeing him again.

Think, Abigail. You want him more than life, and you'll never be happy without him.

No, she refused to weep like a ninny. At least not yet.

She grabbed the laundry in her arms, and hurried up to the first floor.

On the stair landing, she looked out the window.

Out there in the mellow sunlight, wearing no shirt, was Turk. Alone and desirable as sin.

For some reason, he'd stayed behind. She smiled at her good fortune. She wouldn't waste time wondering why she'd been given this chance.

He'd obviously been working hard, his muscled body glistened with sweat. She curled her fingers tighter around the laundry in her excitement.

She licked her lips, able to taste his salt on her tongue. A shiver of pleasure raced over her body.

Hurry. He's out there and he's alone. Hurry.

The fresh clothing she'd been carrying was flung across the bed in her haste to make herself ultra- desirable.

A spritz of perfume, a soft pink prairie skirt and the tightest white pullover she owned completed her fashion statement. Whipping a brush through her hair left it looking like a spun brunette web framing her flushed face.

She tripped and tumbled onto the bed, but rolled easily onto her feet to jam them into a pair of turquoise moccasins. A liberal amount of pink lip-gloss was applied as she ran down the stairs and out the front door.

Find your cowboy.

Outside, the wind was cool, and made her nipples pucker. Or was it the desire to be with him?

The damage around her was hard to ignore, especially since she felt responsible for all of it. She hesitated. Had she lost her mind completely? He had to feel nothing but rage every time he looked around his property. Or, what was left of it.

Momentary doubt slowed her step toward what she craved.

Abigail, you're running out of time.

He can't know what you want if you waste time out here.

Squaring her shoulders, she went confidently inside the ancient looking shed with its bleached boards and rusted tin roof.

She couldn't see him, just sensed him in the warm, gloomy interior.

Muffled thumping sounds in another part of the structure were softened by bales of straw and walls lined with finely decorated tack.

The sun filtered inside through the half open door on slanted rays and played through the ancient streamers of dust. She put out her hand to catch the warmth in her fingers.

"What are you doing in here?"

She spun to find him gazing at her, a hint of a knowing smile on his face. That didn't weaken her desire to make him admit he wanted her. If only for the afternoon.

Joyful heat rippled through her body at the sight of him, just hearing his low, drawling words. Feminine know-how whispered in her ear. Tell him what you want.

"Looking for you."

He took a step closer, observing her through narrowed eyes. "Go back to the house."

"Why?" She'd backed into bales of straw and used them to keep her balance. "We need to talk."

He used his shirt to slowly wipe down his chest and flat stomach, and dry his hair before tossing the shirt on the bale next to her.

"That isn't why you came out here." He casually unbuckled his belt and pulled it from his jeans. "Is it?"

What now? This wasn't meant to be his party. He was supposed to be on his knees, begging for morsels.

That could still happen if she didn't melt like a candle in his heat.

"So, you're able to read my thoughts now?" The soft tease in her voice wasn't intentional, simply impossible to stop.

"Like a cheap novel." He eyed her with a speculative smile.

The word cheap was right on target, stinging her heart so badly she sucked in a breath.

She was on the verge of crying, but held it in. He wouldn't have the pleasure of knowing he'd hurt her.

"You like cheap things if I recall your daring exploits at that sleazy bar." Her eyes burned with a combination of angry, unshed tears and a battered heart. "I've tried talking sensibly, but you can't reason with a deranged ass."

"Ms. Van Huffington. If you don't want sex, get the hell out of here. Now."

His vulgar words were a potion of indescribable visions and sensory thrills, jump-starting her libido.

Just like that, fingers of erotic delight worked their way over every sensitive nerve of her body, slipping coyly into the damp, pulsing spot between her legs.

"Your mind is filthy, Turk." She evaded his hand that reached for hers. "I thought we might carry on a decent conversation. Not rut like one of your cheap Blue Balls girls."

"We can talk while we rut." He reached for her again, and her blood went on a hot rampage. "Talk's cheap. Fucking costs a hell of a lot, baby."

The gleam in his eyes was so damned explicit in its bawdy message, how was she supposed to appear bored?

You should be slapping his face, not working up a climax.

Nip this in the bud. He's having too much fun.

"That's your most endearing quality." Evading him was becoming more difficult. She skipped away to press against the far wall, the urge to run into his arms stealing her willpower. "Can't you form a sentence that isn't comprised of four letter words?"

"That isn't what you want, lady." He hooked his thumbs in the waist of his jeans and looked her up and down. "Hop up on those bales and I'll give it to you."

What now? You've stupidly worked yourself into a trap. It couldn't be better.

She scowled at him. "I will not." Her gaze slid to the bales and checked out the possibility of doing exactly as he suggested. "I wanted to be adult about this, but you're forcing me to your level."

"Oh, I know what level you like." He leaned close, breathing in the scent of her hair. "As deep as I can go."

Her body reacted with quivering defeat the moment he stepped forward, so close his chin grazed her forehead.

He didn't touch her. He didn't have to while the scent of erotic maleness robbed her of all sensibility.

"I don't find you the least bit attractive when you talk like a smelly field hand."

You're a miserable example of womanhood, Abigail. He knows you're ready to pull his jeans down to his ankles.

He moved in, grazing her breasts with his body, looking over her shoulder as he strummed the chords of her erogenous zone. "I think you like making it with this filthy field hand." His voice deepened, laced with urgency. "You seem to get real excited by the things I do. Bring any jelly with you?"

He's working you into being a willing accomplice to him taking off your undies.

That's right. You aren't wearing any.

Make him ask for whatever he gets. Oh, damn it. She'd be begging any minute now.

She took one last swing at his macho attitude.

"Turk, I understand your anger and embarrassment about last night, but that doesn't mean we can't still be friends." *Look at him. He doesn't give a damn what you say.* "I want to leave only pleasant memories."

Her subtle insult drew no response. He obviously wasn't perturbed by her words.

He shifted his weight, leaving her no escape, and licked his lips.

Did he want to taste her?

The low burning flame in her body wouldn't be stamped down too much longer. His scent took her back into his bed, replaying every nip and kiss, every thrust and sigh.

She stiffened with expectation as he touched the soft fabric of her skirt, rolling the material between his thumb and finger.

"I like that," he murmured.

Don't you dare shiver or close your eyes. But, he smells so good. Was that whining?

She stood trembling, helpless to react against his fingers twisting in the hem of her Tee-shirt. Nothing could be done to stop the tingling line he drew across her bare skin until it ended under the curve of her breast.

"Did you hear what I said?"

Of course he did and doesn't believe you. He tilted his head, the angle shadowing her face.

"You're wasting time. What do you really want?"

"I want you."

The words came from the most carefully-guarded secret place in her heart.

He didn't say the words she'd hoped for, his mouth smiling speculatively while the passion in his eyes swept away all silly need to be reassured.

"I think we're going to set this shed on fire, Huffy."

"We should begin putting out the flame right now."

All the wise and wicked plans she'd brought with her were squashed under his boot. She cared less now that he'd won the skirmish, wanted her senses set aflame by his firm mouth closing over hers in a hard, wet kiss, his moan speaking clearly of his desire.

He stumbled forward, pressing her to the wall, ignoring the shower of bridles and lead lines that rained down over them.

She had lost her will, clinging to him with a muffled cry of happiness. Closing her eyes, she murmured against his lips. "Lets take today."

In Turk's strong arms, she couldn't remember the cruel taunts she'd planned for him. She didn't care about that, only the heartbreaking excitement of being in love.

Lost in a vaporous sensuality, she drifted in desire so vivid, her body quaked under his caress. She scraped her nails across his muscled back while her tongue lapped adoringly at his small nipples.

He sucked in his breath and gripped her arms tightly. "You little cat."

"You're my cowboy." Her laugh was husky with passion. "Are you wearing spurs?"

His reaction was a new jolt of pheromone to her blood. In a smooth motion, his hand was under her skirt, moving up between her thighs.

She gasped with pleasure, grabbing at his hand to slide it to her aching center. She had no intention of stopping his progress. Instead, she pressed it closer to her quivering flesh.

"My God, baby, you sure as hell don't wear many clothes." His Texas drawl was pronounced and sexy as hell, teasing her just like his hands that knew no boundary. "You know how to mess me up, don't you?"

He cupped her hips in his hands, pulling her close. The heated bulge against her belly left no question as to his desire.

"If you're too messed up, I'll have to help you, cowboy."

Her hands shook with excitement, her fingers nimbly freeing the buttons on his fly.

How was she to think straight and with his fingers inside her, sliding in and out to bring her closer to climax. She shook with anticipation.

Dipping her hand inside the hot pouch that carried his all man package, Abigail hesitated for the briefest second after she heard the chiding words of her inner woman' voice.

He doesn't love or want you, Abigail.
Go away!

Stopping was not possible. Turk was all she wanted, and if getting him meant barring her soul, nothing was too much to ask.

She freed her prize and gazed in victorious delight at it. He was hot and pulsing in her hand. "You're just right, Turk." Drops of moisture on his tip provided a wonderful, sensuous lube for the lovely silken head. "Pick me up, cattle rustler. Fit me onto your beautiful saddle horn."

He gently squeezed her clit and spoke in his beautiful, husky sex voice. "I want to kiss your sweet little box." His breathing was labored, the violent beat of his heart against her breast sounded almost dangerous.

He carried her to the saddle rail and set her on the precarious perch, tossing her skirt over her head.

She grabbed the support columns on either side of her and shrieked with delight.

The man's an animal and you love it.

He pushed her legs apart and pulled them over his shoulders.

The first brush of his face with its half days beard, scraped the inside of her thighs and shot her into orbit.

She was certain she was going to die.

Chapter 27

Turk loved the beautiful female things about her. Even her shrieks meant Huffy was having a good time, and he sure as hell loved giving her pleasure.

She smelled of exotic flowers and heart-stopping woman's scent that made him hard as the barrel of his rifle. Satin smooth, delicate and wet with passion's dew.

The lady gripped his face between her thighs and pushed her butt closer.

He opened her lips to tease the swollen nub peeking out from her glistening folds. Alluring female fragrance overwhelmed his senses with its perfume.

Turk closed his eyes to absorb every little nuance of what he was doing, every tiny gasp elicited from her soft mouth.

With slow deliberation, he flicked his tongue over the small pink jewel, nipping the petite mound with his teeth.

The way she wiggled hit him with a massive dose of erotic pleasure.

Think of ways to please her.

She moaned as his tongue dipped inside her hot slit, lifted her tight little ass up off the rail while he nibbled and tongued her clit.

Her cry of ecstasy was more than he could stand. His hand shook holding his own cock, driving him wild, trying to guide himself inside her. He'd done this more times than he could remember, but with Huffy, it was the first damn time, every time.

Sweet heaven!

His tip found the slick entrance to complete happiness, and his mouth fused with hers. He licked her lips and tongue wanting to share the nectar he'd just devoured.

Her small opening tightened. She almost toppled from the rail.

Damn, baby." He didn't recognize his own voice, the raspy sound seemed far away. "I love fucking you, Huffy."

There were much more he wanted to tell her, dangerous words that took his breath just to be thinking them.

I love what you make me feel. I love you, Abigail.

His thoughts had to have been picked up by her woman's sensors. She climaxed in a rage, screaming his name and bucking against him as if he was her last hope for life.

Oh the hot, sweet pleasure of coming with Huffy. Sounds of splintering glass and tolling bells rolled through his brain, nothing mattered in the world except being inside her sweet body and fucking her again. He came, the process almost too painful from all the passion he spent with it.

Tears streamed down her flushed cheeks and she whispered those killer words.

"I love you so much, Turk." In her passion, she kissed his face and mouth, hugging him fiercely.

He was shook to the core. She loved him.

God, he wanted that, but knew she wasn't ready for what he had to offer.

A modest, rural life with a dull ex-Ranger would lose its appeal damn fast. He didn't have to guess about his reaction if she stayed and then changed her mind. He couldn't take the loss.

Huffy needed to spread her wings, taste life on her own before settling down with a guy who loved staying home rather than hitting the bars.

He chose teasing over the hard truth. "You love me?"

His legs nearly buckled when she answered. "Yes, with my very life."

He hugged her tight, dreading the tears that were surely coming. "You'll do a hell of a lot better than me, Huffy. Some young guy is waiting out there with a great future. You deserve some body like that, not a worn out old man."

Looking into her eyes tore out his heart. He'd hurt her and he hated himself with the deepest sting.

"No, no." She sobbed, clinging to him. "I don't want anyone but you. I never will!" In her frustration, she slapped him. "Don't talk to me this way. How can you be so cruel?"

"I'm being honest, baby." He took her from the rail she'd sat on. "Try to see the truth."

"You want me, Turk. Want me bad, but something in you tells you to be cruel. Won't let it happen."

"I didn't say I didn't want you. How can you doubt it?" Turk pulled the hem of her T-shirt down to cover her sleek belly. "I'd only hold you back. I'm trying to save us both some hell somewhere down the road."

Her strangled sob cut through him like hot lead. He'd never liked women's tears, but Huffy's sobs would haunt him forever. The touch of her slender body rocked him. She was trembling head to toe. He'd done this and still she clutched at his shoulders with desperation.

"Don't make me leave," she whispered. "I won't cause any hell. I'll never want more than we have."

He took her hands away from his shoulders, looked to heaven for help. None came. "You'll feel differently later, baby."

She pulled away, and gazed at him, her smooth brow creased with emotion. Her sweet voice twisted his heart. "I wish you could love me, Turk." She pushed away from him.

She spun and ran from the shed in a flurry of pink skirts and damp brunette curls.

"Huffy."

His call was too little, too late.

I do love you, baby.

He hadn't had time to get his nerves even into rag-tag order before Gun and Ram came roaring back to the house.

He didn't want to think about law, corrals, or barns right now. His ears still roared and his stomach rolled with tension.

The dust hadn't settled before ram made one of his sensible comments.

"We're going to rope a couple of your nags and round up the rest of the herd." He pointed with pride to the makeshift corral they'd all worked on earlier that morning. "That should hold them for a while."

"Sounds like a deal." Turk struggled to button his shirt. "Did the sheriff have anything new to say?"

"What have you been doing while we were gone?" Gun's knowing smile irritated Turk.

"Straightening feed sacks in the...aw hell. What do you care?" Turk sensed horseplay was coming.

"It looks like a three year old buttoned your shirt and your face is red.

Been hot?" Gun's brow lifted knowingly.

"I really don't want any crap from you." Turk went back in the shed to grab his hat. "Stop yapping and lets round up those cayoose."

* * * *

Abigail staggered under the weight of her emotions and ran from the man she adored and up the stairs to her room.

One all consuming feeling gripped her complete being.

She hated him.

Needing a place to hide, she tore the soiled clothing off and fled to the bathroom to cry it out.

For a long while, she stood in the showers full blast icy spray, hating herself more than the object of her recent fury.

Finally, wrung out and shaking with cold, she climbed from the shower and wrapped a bath sheet around her shaking body.

She sank to the floor, waiting for the hurt to ease.

Everything she'd done while at the lodge haunted her. Everything had been so wrong. She'd made a fool of herself and this time, her impetuous ways left a lifelong scar on her heart.

None of that mattered now. After a final visit to the hospital to see Shane, she'd be on her way to Puerta Vallarta.

Abigail wanted to pour out her troubles to her grandmother while they talked on the hone, but that was out of the question. The drama of her lost love would hold no interest to the rest of the world.

Thank goodness for her loving grandmother. She'd been delighted to hear her only granddaughter and would immediately take care of the reservations for her travel.

Now, she'd not have to suffer begging money from Turk. That would be too humiliating.

Abigail pushed aside the hurtful despair that hung over her as Lucy slipped from the closet. The kittens must be full and napping for their mother to leave them long enough for her own daily pampering.

Inhaling roughly with unshed tears, Abigail picked up Lucy, holding her for a few minutes. She carried the cat to the window, looking out at the deserted front yard.

The huge silver and black truck that the rest of the Gunnison clan had arrived in was parked near the tack shed.

She wondered where the men had gone. It was too quiet without their male voices and noise.

The wait wasn't long before the quiet burst with their arrival. She stopped packing to listen to the distant rumble, the sound gaining in volume.

Opening the window, she saw the first of the horses gallop into the yard. They were back.

Lucy stared at the window for a moment, then turned tail and ran for the closet.

Coming up the lane was the rest of the herd that had scattered during the horrible shoot out.

She found Turk in the wild-west show astride his big, black horse, waving his Stetson to keep the horses running ahead.

She couldn't help the way she warmed just looking at him, her real live cowboy. Handsome and unattainable.

Ram raced alongside the herd, twirling a rope over his head in a wide loop, his smile big as the state of Texas.

Riding a wide circle around them, Gun galloped toward the front of the herd to the new corral they had made. He waited for the horses to run inside the temporary pen.

They closed the milling animals in with several poles across the entrance, and then removed their horse's saddles.

After a few moments, Abigail realized she'd been daydreaming over the lovely scene below. Here she was, staring out from behind the curtains like a Nervous Nelly.

Go back to work. There had been no need worrying she'd be noticed. The men immediately set to work watering and feeding the animals, completely comfortable in their world of chores and ribald laughter.

She moved away from the window. Temptation whispered in her ear, but she brushed it away, concentrated on cleaning out drawers and clearing shelves instead of foxy ways to seduce Turk.

Soon, the wastebaskets were overflowing with the items she'd never want to see again. Her heart lurched when the red lounge outfit hit the discarded pile.

No more whining. That was just a reminder of her ridiculous love affair in which she'd apparently been the only one in love.

She kicked the overflowing container.

Fighting anger and hurt, she tossed the last of her cosmetics into a leather makeup case.

The irony of owning such an expensive variety of makeup was huge.

She sighed, remembering she hadn't applied makeup very often while living at the lodge.

One more way to lose a man's interest.

Blaming a lack of makeup was ridiculous. She had only herself to blame.

Chapter 28

Avoiding Turk wasn't hard.

Abigail spent most of the day alone in the house while the men ran back and forth into town for supplies, and she knew they'd gone to Blue Balls at least once.

Turk had carried a large white shirt box into his office. He'd finally broken down and bought new ones. She wished now that she'd sewn all those missing buttons on for him.

Gun had made sandwiches for them at lunch and sat with her on the patio while she ate hers. She knew he was there to enjoy his cigar, not keep her company.

She had tried to avoid developing any feelings for them, but she liked Turk's brothers.

Gun was obviously mad for his wife, Ali and their four children. She wanted to hug him when he dragged out his picture gallery again, beaming as she said lots of complimentary things about his beautiful wife and babies.

From his splintered picnic table, Turk watched them, and smiled at her.

Oh, no you don't cowboy. That smile no longer works.

Gun stood, his words soft and easy. "Can't you give him a break? He can't help being a little stupid." He left her to finish the coffee he'd brought out. The brew was wonderful, strong and rich in color. Reminiscent of Turk, the way his skin glowed in the evening sun and strong like his arms.

Oh sure, everything those men did was unforgettable.

She got to her feet and went in the house, dreading the inevitable moment she would come face-to-face with Turk, yet longing for it.

Seized by a restless fever to be busy, she spent several hours cleaning her bathroom and changed her bed linen.

She allowed tears to fall when the vacuum covered any sound of her crying.

Would she ever make right choices again? Not as long as she could feel Turk's presence.

Taking a minute to peek at Lucy's babies, Abigail went weak with emotion, knowing how much she was going to miss Turk and everything about the lodge.

Closing the closet door some to allow the cat her privacy, she checked to make sure she'd left out enough clothing for a trip to the hospital and then to Puerta Vallarta.

Now, there was nothing left.

"Abigail. Come on down." It was Ram, his friendly voice coaxing. "We're all going to Blue Ball's."

She bristled.

She couldn't be angry with Ram. He didn't know his brother was a toad and had a handy bed partner at that place.

"No thank you."

"You can't stay here alone." Ram's voice softened. "Please."

She sighed. "I'm sorry, Ram." What could she say? "I think I'm coming down with a cold. Anyway, I have to press some things."

Silence.

What was going on among the three charmers downstairs?

"Can we bring you anything?" Gun's drawling words almost changed her mind, but not quite.

"No. I'm good. A cup of hot tea. Then bed and I'll be fine." She forced a cough. "Thanks anyway."

She heard the front door open and close, and one of those big trucks started and drove away.

She was alone.

Accepting the fact she was a coward, Abigail looked down into the entry hall, checking to see if one of the men had stayed behind. God, she wished they had. Being alone in this big old squeaky house amplified her every fear.

Inhaling over the knot in her stomach, she hitched up her nerve.

No use idly sitting around until the men returned. She'd seen a novel on Turk's nightstand.

It would be impossible to sneak anywhere in this house. The stairs creaked and groaned from top to bottom under her feet.

The office door was open. That always meant he was out. She was going in.

The scent of his libido-heating cologne rushed out to kiss her lips and quickened her pulse.

Hurry, idiot. You might do crazy things like crawl all over his bed.

The book wasn't on his desk. He must have taken it to the bedroom.

Inside his pleasure palace, he might as well have been lolling on that massive bed of feather and down. His presence filled every corner, pursuing her as she searched for the book.

The allusive novel had been tossed onto his comfy club chair by the window.

Grab the damn book and run!

Leaving wasn't that simple. How was she to stop the soft thrumming of her heart?

Pleasure and love had bloomed in this room.

She gazed at the bed, warmed with the sweet memories. Passion and love.

Her eyes flew open.

A car door. She'd dallied too long.

If Turk found her in his room, he'd assume she was too weak to stay away from him.

Well, aren't you?

With the pilfered book in hand, she raced from his lair. She stopped long enough to grab a handful of the jellybeans from the glass decanter.

Plop—plop. Dang it.

She dropped candy with every step.

No need to worry about that.

Turk was to full of himself to notice a pretty jellybean under his boot.

* * * *

Turk knew she'd been in his room. The scintillating perfume of warm flowers always followed her.

What had she been doing in there?

Nothing was disturbed.

His heart pounded against his ribs.

She wanted him.

His shoulders slumped.

Don't be a fool. She hates you.

Out in the hall, he'd found a rainbow of candy, scattered across the floor and up half the stairs.

She'd been running to avoid him.

He ached with disgust, knowing he must rank right up there with pond scum in Huffy's eyes.

He'd always regret the way things ended between them.

Maybe if he tried to explain again.

Don't be a fool.

She might weaken for one moment and you'd fall into that abyss headfirst and wind up drowning. No!

She's leaving and you're okay with that.

Turk wanted to yell. No, he was not okay.

Picking up a pastel candy, he wondered how in the hell his life had gotten so turned around and always in a frenzy of things he couldn't control.

He looked at the busted up wood and glass around him.

Images of what he'd been damn good at flickered in his mind like a bad movie.

Weapons and hardship. No one to answer to but his men. No, he didn't want that again. Maybe the CIA or FBI.

Inhaling hard to deaden the ache, he glanced up the stairs, dreading tomorrow as much as he'd ever dreaded anything.

Get out of the house.

Suck it up and face this. You're not leaving.

Huffy is.

God, why did it hurt so bad?

He was lost, unsure of which way to turn.

His unsympathetic brother's were in the great room. He could hear them laughing. Damn. Did the TV have to be turned up so loud? One of them obviously had hearing issues.

He dragged himself into the room and gazed around. The scene was straight out of the past.

Gun sprawled all over the best and most comfortable couch in the house. Ram lay back, taking his ease in the only recliner Turk used to watch television.

They barely looked up when he entered the room.

Gun pulled himself up on an elbow to drag his cell phone from his belt. Wanting privacy, he went to the library table, taking notes as he listened.

Ram yawned and tossed the week old paper he'd been reading on the coffee table. "I'll drive Abigail to the airport in the morning. It's no trouble since I plan to hop a flight out of here myself."

Turk scowled at him. "When did this all happen?"

"Yesterday." The smile on Ram's face was Cheshire style. "Before your last falling out."

"Fine." What was he supposed to say to that? "I'll be too busy getting this place rebuilt to waste time playing chauffeur."

The look Gun shot his way made the hair on Turk's neck bristle. "Don't pop a vein, brother." He went back to his conversation.

Okay. Keep it cool. No need to let them leave in a bad mood or with something else to hold over his head. "Let's have a beer and play some five card stud." He broke out a fresh deck, looking forward to winning a few hands. "Come, on Gun. I'm taking you both to the cleaners."

They sat at the round oak table, drinking their beers and eating peanuts and pretzels.

Bad idea.

Turk could see Huffy laying back on the table, jelly on her breasts and passion in her blue eyes.

Gun saved the moment. His phone rang.

Turk left the room to stand in the entry hall.

Was he ever going to make it through a day in one piece?

Ah, the nights. Torture like he'd never endured. He knew it was coming.

A soft cough from the stair landing tore open his already bleeding heart. "Turk."

His heart cried out a flowery ode to her, but he slashed it down.

"Huffy. Can I help you?"

"I need to use the phone." She stepped down one stair, her expression wary. "To call my employer. Is that all right?"

Sure!

Go ahead. Make your plans and don't look at me.

"Sure, it's okay." He started to leave.

Gun looked out at them, pointing to the phone. "I gotta hit the road, Turk. Ali isn't feeling well."

"Noting serious is it?" Turk was concerned about his sister-in-law.

Gun had already started up the stairs to get his things. "Not sure. New baby and all. She never complains, so this is more than usual."

Ram came out, a slight frown on his face. "Anything I can do, Gun?"

"Just get Abigail to the airport on time and maybe make sure Turk has all his marbles in one bag. He's unusually nervous lately."

In less than two minutes, Gun was back down the stairs, duffle in one hand and his keys in the other. He ran back up the steps to hug Huffy. "When you get tired of England, come on down to Dallas. Ali's going to love having you around."

She was right behind him, tying the belt of her bathrobe. "I hope she's okay."

* * * *

Abigail followed the men to the door and watched the brother's hug as they said their goodbyes.

No matter how loud their conversations, they loved one another.

Gun drove away, the red taillights of his truck swallowed up by the dark after he rounded the curve where the huge boulders stood.

She hadn't noticed before, but a fine mist had begun to fall.

Turk brushed at his hair and bunched his shoulders. The air was chilly and seeped through the soft material of her robe.

Turk and Ram talked for several minutes before turning to come to the house.

She quickly went to the phone, not wanting them to know she'd been watching them.

While she thumbed through the pages of her address book, Abigail realized the time difference between London and Lone Horse was too vast to make a call that night. It would have to wait.

"Something wrong?" Turk stood behind her.

"No." She tried to swallow, but her throat was too dry. "I'll call tomorrow."

He obviously would still jump in bed with her, his yes stroking her breasts as he spoke. "We'll head for Denver around noon tomorrow. If you need anything, we can pick it up there."

"No." She turned to escape the longing that dropped like fine netting over her. "I'll be ready when you want to leave."

He caught her arm, slowing her retreat. "I don't want things to be ugly between us."

"Don't ask me to be friends, Turk." She detested the weak sound of her voice. But, most of all, she hated the ache in her heart.

"We're more than friends." He brushed his chin against her forehead. "I'm—are you going to be okay? Over there?"

"You pick a hell of a time to express concern about my future." Resentment clouded her attempt at decorum. "I'll simply pick up where I left off. Without you."

Why did he have to look so contrite when she knew he wasn't in the least? Must he stand so near?

His male vibes radiated through the work-worn shirt on his strong back.

She teetered toward him like a moth to the flame.

"Let me drive you to the airport."

"I wouldn't think of it."

"You're being childish."

"Something you could never adjust to."

"I don't want you thinking like that."

"Why not?" She stopped short of flaying him with a choice, colorful name. Ram had stumbled into hearing distance of their conversation, backing up when he noticed them. She whispered her last barb. "You're in the clear, Mister Gunnison. I won't haunt your dreams."

Chapter 29

Turk had hit the floor that morning ahead of sunup, showered and dressed before the first bleary rays stabbed through the gray clouds that morning.

At half past eleven, the clatter of dishes on the floor made him turn away from the window. Lucy waited by her bowl. She had learned to paw the empty dish to get his attention. She eyed the fancy giblets he spooned out for her.

"You were maybe expecting caviar?" He patted her head. "You're getting plump, lady."

Outside, leaves from the aspens fluttered by the windows and piled up on the wrecked glider.

Damn. He wasn't ready for dismal winter weather.

The scene in the kitchen was pretty dreary too. Ram sat at the table with Huffy, practically hand feeding her tater-tots.

It was almost noon and she'd managed to avoid him all day.

Longing to be part of her circle pushed him to the cozy picture. She glanced his way as he sat down.

Turk didn't mind breaking up the party. "We should head out pretty soon."

Her gaze fluttered over him, and then moved to the food on her plate. He thought of butterflies. Flowers by the stable. Sweet lilac and strawberry preserves.

"I'll get my handbag." She daintily wiped her fingers on the napkin Ram handed her. "I want to pick up some flowers and books for Shane." Her eyes narrowed. "That's if you don't mind."

This was the real Huffy. Acid tongue and evil temper.

"Of course, I don't mind." He knew better, but couldn't help himself. With a flick of a napkin, he cleaned a speck of crusty potato from the corner of her mouth. "Tater. Tot. On your mouth."

Ram chuckled. *Damn.* The man always seemed to be around when he made blunders with Huffy.

"Thank you for the mop up." She grabbed the napkin from his nervous hand. "Shall I bathe or am I good to roll, as you say?"

"I'll wait in the truck."

She stalked from the kitchen, leaving a trail of female angst and bewitching perfume.

What did he do before falling in love with Huffy? Lived a very dull life.

He listened to his brother, but didn't turn around. With his case of heartache, he didn't want to talk to anyone.

"Are you listening to me?"

"Yeah, I heard you, Ram." He took his truck keys from the wall hook. "The builders will be here in the morning. The stable won't be anything like the original, but it'll keep the animals dry until I can rebuild the way I want it."

Ram stood next to him. "Wish I could stay longer, but I have orders to get to Florida ASAP."

"Don't worry about it." Here it was now, ice cold and ugly. The truth. He was going to be alone for the next two months. He'd become used to being alone, but that was before Huffy. "I'll have this finished by the time you come back. There's nothing to get in my way."

"Yeah, well--." Ram inhaled and stared ahead. "You need to think that over, brother."

No time to tell him to mind his own business. Huffy came down the steps and charged out the door. Ram grinned and went back to the kitchen.

Out in the truck, Huffy fastened her seatbelt only after he pointed to it and gazed at her until she got the message.

Finally, they were off and running like a pack of hounds were after them. God, he despised being alone with a pissed off woman. Especially when he was right.

She set him straight pretty damn quick after he hit a chug hole in the road.

"Slow down and you need to get glasses Grandpa."

Damn, it was great to hear her voice, even if she was cussing him. "I'll do that."

He couldn't help but look at her, and recognized the spiffy white suit and matching snap brimmed straw hat. The netting and Guinea hen feathers were just jaunty enough for her pouty little face. She'd been wearing it the day she'd arrived at Lone Horse.

She caught his stare and looked away. No sir, not a crumb for him.

Face it, Gunnison. You deserve all of the crap she tosses your way. You should have sent her on her way like she wanted. You are the dumbest man when it comes to her.

She stands you on your head and you love it.

You love her.

The softest sigh he'd ever heard flowed from her lips and he wanted to pull over and kiss her. Would she sit next to him on the way home? Maybe if he... *No, bite the bullet and own up to your fate.*

Thank God, traffic picked up and the hospital was a couple blocks down the road. He needed something to take his mind off the one thing that would cause him grief the rest of his life.

His beautiful Arizona rose.

* * * *

"Pull into that strip mall." Abigail made up her mind during their ride, she wasn't too proud to beg for her friend. "There's a nice florist shop that looks like it carries books and gifts for patients as well."

Turk nodded obligingly and wheeled into the crowded parking lot.

She held out her hand and he stared mutely for a split second.

"Oh, okay." He dug out his wallet and handed her his credit card. "Want me to go with you?"

"Maybe you should. They may question my name being Turk."

He got out and followed her into the shop, looking uncomfortable next to the frilly bed jackets and nightgowns.

She was surprised to see him pick up a pair of pink booties. Fat chance he'd ever have anything smaller than a colt to put them on.

Stop looking at him.

He just ripped your heart to shreds and you're having baby thoughts.

She forced her gaze from him to focus on the get-well cards. A cute one with puppies would do.

Flowers were next on order. A huge bouquet of white daisies and pink iris caught her eye.

"I'll take those and that large box of candy." She plopped Turk's card down on the counter.

He added a stack of magazines to the purchases.

"Those aren't biker magazines are they?" She scanned the covers, seeing nothing but sports figures and fast cars. "Okay. We'll take those as well."

She boldly signed the sales receipt and then handed the card to Turk.

Nice, compliant, handsome Turk. What woman wouldn't fall for this sexy guy right out of the Old West?

As much as it hurt to admit, she still wanted him like an addict needed a fix. He was her drug, had always taken her to the heights of passion.

You're a fool, Abigail.

He'd done all that and then dropped you over the cliff with no net waiting to catch you.

She still wept inside.

"Abigail."

Her head jerked up in surprise. "Why so formal? I prefer the lowlife name you stuck on me."

"I have to say this. I'm feeling like hell." He opened the door of the truck. "I—I'm going to miss you."

"You'll have Blue Balls to help you with that."

"Damn it, Huffy."

"Turk. There's no legitimate reason for you to speak to me again unless it pertains to my leaving." She ached to slap him for good measure. "Let's go. Shane is probably lonely."

"He's not the only one." Turk slammed the door after she'd climbed in the truck. He got in, glaring at her. "Think you can sweeten that tongue of yours? Shane will have a fatal relapse if he gets a dose of that viper's sting."

"Shut up and drive."

* * * *

The flowers smelled sickeningly sweet, and his stomach rolled.

What a fool, fighting with the woman he loved and wanted for all eternity. He was in agony.

In the crowded elevator, he accidentally pressed against Huffy's slender body.

The emotional sting almost sent him to his knees.

They piled out like sardines from a can and he took his first real breath in the last five minutes.

Against her wishes and a hard frown, he took her elbow, guiding her through the maze of carts, life saving equipment and gurneys that choked the hallway.

They found Shane's room and hesitated outside his door. He had company. A tall, slender woman with silver gray hair hovered over him. The man with her was large and had a booming laugh and a shock of steely gray hair.

"His parents." Huffy squared her shoulders and walked into the room.

Turk followed, seeing the resemblance to his parents in Shane's features. Damn, it was great they had come to get him.

Shane glanced up and grinned from ear to ear. "My parents are here. Come meet them."

Turk shook hands with the Caloun's, but the older man was not satisfied with that pansy greeting. He put a killer bear hug on Turk and kissed Huffy on both cheeks.

"Our son talks about nothing but the two of you. I think he wants to be a cowboy."

As expected, Huffy went straight for Shane and planted a dozen kisses on his mouth and face.

The room overflowed with laughter and accented voices and old-fashioned love. Turk learned their names were Irena and Ivan.

Over the din, Ivan told Turk he was taking Shane home in a couple of days. "He's so proud to be your friend, Mr. Gunnison. We owe you a great deal."

Turk squirmed at such praise. "You don't owe me anything. Shane's a brave man and helped me out of a jam."

Huffy looked up, her blue eyes shadowed by sooty lashes. He was sure she saw him as a witless goatherd.

She turned her back and held court in Russian.

He recalled now, she'd tried to tell him about her life, her job, but he'd cut her off. Huffy was educated, smart and going places. Without him.

He listened to the impossible language that to spilled from her sweet tongue. During a brief lull, he offered a bit of inane conversation. "Uh, Shane." *Okay, time to scuff your toe on the floor, idiot.* "What's your plan? You coming back to Lone Horse?"

"Not yet." The enthusiasm in the kid's eyes reminded him of himself a long time ago. "I'm going back to school and get that full degree in political science and law. I'm going into politics."

"That sounds great." Turk rubbed the back of his neck. He was tense. *My god, you dread being alone with Huffy.* "You'll do a great job, probably be the youngest Supreme Court judge in history."

Shane would have made a hell of a military man. He was tough as nails and could take a hell of a beating.

Turk couldn't help grinning. The kid was a babe magnet as well. Three different nurses came in to check his blood pressure and fluff his pillows.

"Hey, Turk." The pampered patient bit into another chocolate. "Abbey said she'd get us cheap airfare and we could stay with her in London. We'd have a blast."

He was a dead man.

Huffy's head rotated like an owl's and her eyes dared him to say something stupid.

"Yeah." He had to say something. "We'll do that sometime."

The look she gave him conveyed a powerful, ball busting message. She never wanted to see him again.

Forty-five long, sweaty minutes later, Shane wore down and they were asked to leave.

At the door, Turk left Shane an invitation. "Come on back to Lone Horse when you can. I'll always be there."

The deep, cold silence between him and Huffy on the elevator nearly burst his eardrums.

The normal dainty clicking of her heels on the tile floor of the lobby went through his head like a shot.

Sharper yet was her whispered spite.

"That invitation was for Shane alone. Surely you're intelligent enough to know that."

Enough. He held his tongue until they were well on the way back to the lodge. Turk didn't want to exchange more angry words with her.

They closed the door of communication between them.

Turk struggled against the horrible, debilitating feeling of being aloft in the darkening sky. He couldn't concentrate.

Drive, fool. Get back where you know who you are.

Pulling onto the road to the house, he wanted to yell at her to stop being so cold. He knew under all that bluster, she was cut to the quick.

He chose to be cordial, but kept his distance.

Looks like the contractor's here."

Silence.

She grabbed her purse and pulled off her hat, walking stiffly ahead of him. She paused in the entry hall and whispered something.

"I didn't hear what you said, huffy."

As she turned to face him, a diaphanous sprig of sweet lilac released a soft drift of her perfume. Her sweet mouth seemed to quiver slightly.

"I meant that invitation for you, but I knew your refusal would hurt too much."

Chapter 30

Abigail looked around the room she'd called home for a brief whirlwind of time in her life.

In spite of the past few hours, she didn't want to leave. That was silly. The one thing she truly wanted would never to be hers. Turk would be nothing more than a distant, devastating memory soon.

She stood and smoothed the quilt that covered her bed. Her hands shook and she pressed them to the creases of her navy slacks.

With love, she brushed Lucy's hair from the matching jacket and let the tears fall where they may.

The dainty clock on her dresser chimed softly, the fragile china time peace oddly out of place in the rough beamed room. Time to leave. The words stunned her with their finality.

She heard footsteps on the stairs, rousing from her thoughts to grab her purse and sunglasses.

Ram stood out in the hall, and waited until she went down the stairs. He came out of her room shortly with all her luggage. Growing wiser while visiting the lodge, she'd discarded half of what she'd arrived with.

Turk. Where was he?

Her gaze darted from corner to corner, searching for that one beloved face.

The truth closed over her, taking her breath with its cruelty.

Not even a goodbye.

Dear God, how was she to survive this?

"Need a minute, honey?" Ram spoke in his gentleman's way, quiet and assuring. "I'll wait outside."

Oh yes, she needed a long time to recover from Turk's show of indifference, not caring enough to see her on her way. How could he be so cold?

She shook her head and ran from the house, holding all the hurt and tears inside. She had no right involving anyone else.

She waited in Ram's SUV, thinking he wasted valuable time packing her junk in.

At last, he got in and buckled up, looking straight ahead as if he felt her misery.

He sped up once they had cleared the long, winding driveway, his jaw set in a familiar line. He was angry.

That look made her want to sob. She'd caused so much pain and anger in her life, she was getting it all back in spades.

Five minutes out on the county road, Ram seemed to be spending an excessive amount of time looking in the rearview mirror.

Now what? The big shiny vehicle seemed be dying a horrible death, coughing and lurching, bucking ahead and then backfiring.

"Can't you make this thing go faster?" She couldn't hide the sob that went with the desperate question. "Please."

"Sorry, Abigail." He fiddled with things on the dash the SUV lurched ahead before stopping cold. "I'll see what's going on."

He opened the door and stepped out, going to the back of the automobile. She couldn't help her reaction, she had to scream out her anger.

"What are you doing? The motor is in the front."

Her heart leapt into her throat. The door opened and two strong arms pulled her from the seat.

"Baby."

No use holding them back now, her sobs drifted off in the cold wind and her heart burst all over again.

She was in Turk's arms, his kiss claiming her with its sweet, hard familiarity. She hugged his neck with all her strength, fingers deep in his hair, holding on to her beloved, her very life.

"Turk." She talked but knew it was all a sobbing ramble. "I was so afraid you wouldn't come for me." He held her so tight she ached. No, that was the pain of rejection.

"Do you want me to stay?" God, please let him say yes.

His gaze lingered on her face, never leaving while he broke her heart again. "I couldn't let you leave without saying goodbye."

What was he doing, finishing tearing out her soul? "Turk! Don't you love me at all?"

"Huffy, I'll love you until my last second on earth." He kissed her deep then, his firm lips clinging to hers with the heat of passion and honesty. "I'm not an easy man to put up with."

"I want you for the rest of my days." She'd stopped crying, her heart began beating again. "I love you Turk, and that will never change. No matter what you say or expect, I'll still be in love with you if I live an eternity."

Strands of hair had escaped the twist at her nape, and moved in the wind. He brushed them from her forehead. "That's what I want, Huffy. Forever." He kissed her again, staggering off into the grassy ditch, so caught up in his show of devotion, holding her up off the wet marsh in his pursuit of the scorching kiss he placed on her lips. "Give it three months, baby, three months to be sure this is what you want."

Here came the tears again. "Three months? That's forever!"

"Huffy! If it's right, you'll know it. I don't want a little of your life, I want it to be for all time."

He took her arms from his shoulders and she immediately hugged them about his waist. He cupped her face in his hands and kissed her hard.

"Turk, I don't want to do this." She touched the curve of his jaw. "It's too much."

She couldn't stop him from moving her back a step to walk her to the truck. Hurt crowded around her again and wouldn't be pushed aside.

"Remember I love you, Huffy."

"I can't do it. You'll forget me."

He stepped back and walked away, head down and taking her heart with him. He turned to look at her one final time. "If you feel the same three months from now, I'm coming to get you. Nothing will keep me away."

She ran after him, stopping in defeat when he got in his truck and sped off down the road.

Abigail wished to die.

* * * *

The tears had stopped, leaving Abigail to shiver in the cold of being separated from Turk.

Falling in love wasn't supposed to break your heart.

She'd thought about asking Ram to take her back to the lodge, but pride still ran through her blood.

Being with her lovely grandmother was a joy, but her personal misery dulled her heart to the pleasure.

Adding to her disappointment came disturbing news from the tour agency. Her beginning date had been moved up by three weeks. They would inform her of the exact day.

The phone rang and she leaned forward, hoping that by some miracle Turk was trying to find her.

"Dear." Her grandmother joined her on the shady veranda, carrying her favorite little dog. "You spend too much time alone. What would you say to a shopping trip?"

"I don't think so, Gran." Abigail stood and walked to the fancy wrought iron gate. "Why don't you come to London with me?"

Her grandmother asked the question she dreaded. "Do you love him terribly?"

"I can't tell you how much, Gran." She could hardly speak. "Its so deep and so sweet I can't describe or feel it all at once."

"You'll see him again, my dear." The elderly woman went to her grieving granddaughter. "That kind of love has no end. He'll come for you."

The following days and afternoons droned by, filled with her grandmother's usual tea served in fine bone china cups and poured from polished silver pots.

Her thoughts went to the wheat pattern dishes in the glass front cabinets in Turks kitchen, the old granite cup he favored for his strong black coffee.

Nothing would be right in her life again. How could she have been so stupid, not seeing him from the first moment for the man he truly was? What had she been looking for, unable to see her heart stood before her in a worn Stetson and scuffed boots?

Pixie, the smallest of the dogs eyed her sympathetically, and Abigail picked her up. She'd trotted ahead of Abigail's grandmother who joined her on the patio.

"You're crying again, Abigail." The elegant woman's eyes held concern for her unhappy granddaughter. "Call him."

Horrified at the idea, Abigail shook her head. "I could never do that."

She placed the dog on the flagstone floor where it leaned against her leg. "You don't understand, Gran. I don't think he love's me—not the way I love him." A sob came unbidden, and she covered her face. "I'm afraid he doesn't want me."

"Terrible, long lasting things can happen if someone doesn't take the risk."

They sat in thoughtful silence as evening closed in, heavy with the perfume of exotic flowers and the melancholy strains of a Spanish love song being played on a guitar nearby.

* * * *

How long had it been? Turk stared at the calendar, despairing at the tortoise pace of the days crawling by. Had it only been three weeks?

Get out of here. Don't think.

He jammed his hat on his head, trying his best not to see the small turquoise moccasins abandoned by the grandfather clock.

Outside, he worked furiously to get the ranch back in shape, but at the ringing of the phone, he dropped everything to answer the call. It might be Huffy.

It never was.

He worked hard at trying to keep out of the contractor's hair. The guy worked from sunup to evening, but it seemed nothing was getting done.

The delays were due in part to his frequent, overly critical ways of viewing finished work. He worried the stables wouldn't be finished by the time the first snow blew.

What about his house? The front door still sagged on busted hinges. Turk figured he'd never get the damn thing fixed to his liking.

One good thing had happened during the past few weeks. Cole returned from his vacation and pitched in like a trooper. He'd loaded up all of the horses in a trailer and took them to Blue Balls stable until their new quarters were ready.

He'd been staying at the lodge, helping out with cleaning up around the place and anything that needed taken care of. He was disappointed about missing the gun battle. Turk hoped he never had to fire another gun for the rest of his life.

It was Sunday. So quiet, hickory-nut shell's the squirrels dropped from the trees sounded like a twenty-two firing. Three weeks ago, his life had purpose. Today he went through the motions of survival. He wanted his reason for living back. What was he waiting for? He couldn't wait much longer.

Cole stepped out of the shell of a stable where he'd been sweeping up sawdust. He wiped his forehead and waved. "Turk. How about taking a break? Go have a few beers at Blue Balls?"

Turk shook his head. Getting loaded and bunking with Glenda wasn't going to happen—now or ever again.

"I don't think so, Cole. You go ahead."

Cole laughed and adjusted the crotch of his Levi's. "I spent too much time in that icy stream. Have to get things warmed up again."

Cole took off in a trot and got in his shiny red truck. Turk figured the kid would show up late tomorrow.

Turk drifted toward the tack shed, using the last bit of courage he possessed to go inside.

Memories of passion too hot to ever cool down still buzzed around the small shed, calling to him, slipping around the post she'd held onto, teasing his skin like sweet smelling lace.

My God, will it ever get better?

Fool, you don't get better if you're missing a heart and soul.

He slid his hand up the post, images of Huffy flashing through his mind.

How long had he said? He was a fool. He couldn't take it any longer. *Go ahead and get a flight out of here.*

No. You're not giving her a chance to adjust. That's a damn lie and you know it. You're afraid she's adjusted too well and will tell you to fuck off.

Turk picked up a pink ribbon from the rough plank floor. Touching it to his nose, he reeled with emotion. Persian lilac.

The distant echo of a phone ringing penetrated his private fog of sweet memories.

He looked over his shoulder at the house, torn apart by hope and sure disappointment.

Was it her? Did she need him?

He'd made a fool's bargain and had to deal with it.

Chapter 31

Turk made his flight with no time to spare, still trying to comb his hair into a decent look as the flight attendant asked him if he wanted peanuts.

"No, I just want to get to Mexico in a hurry."

She'd smiled and handed him a small cup of coffee. "We'll do our best."

He didn't engage her in conversation. Only one woman came to mind for that. God help him if she'd taken off already.

He'd been right, and so wrong. Her grandmother had called, sounding a bit angry with him because Abigail was in total misery. She'd hit him in the gut with the description of her granddaughter's heartbreak, all because of him. And what was he going to do about it?

Sitting on a damn tin-can, thirty-five thousand feet in the air, wanting a shot of Jack to get him through the God awful wait. That's what he was doing about it.

What was he going to say to her, how would he tell her he couldn't go through with the separation?

"Sir." The attendant was back. "More coffee?"

"No, thanks." He turned his head and looked out the window.

I love you, Abigail Van Huffington. Please be there.

He knew exactly what he wanted in the future, going over the possibilities as the miles were eaten up and left behind.

If she'd have him, he'd take Huffy home to Dallas, and introduce her to his family. The mental picture pleased him.

They'd have all kinds of help getting arrangements made for their wedding. Every Gunnison had been married in the same church.

His gut clenched with apprehension. Huffy may have seen him as he really was. A waffling fool, too afraid to commit to love when he should have.

Made no difference. He had to try.

* * * *

Abigail took one of her grandmother's shawls, and draped it around her shoulders. The sun had disappeared behind the ancient church across the plaza, and it was cool.

Like most evenings, there were guests enjoying the garden patio, her grandmother providing entertainment with Flamingo dancers.

The music was infectious and Abigail turned to watch the couple strut and flirt, the castanet's magic sound setting her foot tapping.

From nowhere, an image of a passionate tryst on the kitchen table filled her thoughts, and her heart raced with remembered desire.

She turned away and hurried to the end of the garden, stopping at the wrought iron fence to wait out the pain.

Strains of the sensuous music followed her, soft but evocative. She gripped the iron bars in her hands and bit her lip.

An orchid drooping down from an old moss covered planter, reminded her of how love could be. Tender, glorious, and heartbreaking.

"Are you waiting for someone, senorita."

She had lost her mind. No one here had a Texas drawl.

Afraid to look up, she turned, keeping her gaze on the reflection pool. He spoke again and her heart crashed against her ribs.

"I hope it's me."

She gazed at him, taking in the image of the man across the pool. "Turk?"

"Abigail."

Her whisper became a cry of joy as she ran to meet him. In a few strides, he caught her up in his arms, kissing her so passionately her heart stopped beating. He was really holding her, his hands bracing her head for his plundering, possessive kiss, his arms crushing her to his heaving chest.

He brought the ecstasy of his touch, and the way he blocked out the rest of the world when he held her. His firm mouth fit over hers with clean, hard persuasion, and she would never let him go again.

"I was thinking of you, Turk." Her fingers drove through his hair, locking in the cool depths. "Why did you wait so long? I've been so lonely."

She wept again, this time from happiness.

"That won't happen ever again, baby." He kissed her lips roughly, as if he staked his claim, and smoothed her hair. "I've been about crazy without you, Huffy."

He was really here, saying those wonderful things. But, not everything. "I thought about you and the kitchen table, Turk." What was he thinking now? Did she have to draw him pictures?

He groaned, pulling her close. "That damn table's still there, clean as a whistle."

"Look here, Turk." She pushed on his chest, wanting to yell at him for being so dense. "If you don't tell me you love me, you can run back to Lone Horse."

His voice was deep and rough, rich with honesty and tenderness. "I love you, Huffy. If you will, I want you to be my wife, to have my babies. I'm staking my life on you wanting that too." He pulled her back into his arms and whispered against her lips. "I just want one thing in this world, and that's you loving me."

"I loved you from the first day, the first second." Abigail clung to him, overjoyed with the completeness of being with her beloved again. "We'll have lot's of beautiful children, boys and girls. Maybe six or seven."

"Time's getting away from us, baby." He placed his palm on her stomach. "The tack shed is in good shape."

"I like the table better."

He hugged and kissed her alternately as he led her from the dark patio, and toward their future. "I just happen to have a fresh supply of strawberry preserves."

"Good. I wouldn't want to have to send you out in the middle of the night to shop at Blue Balls for our pleasure toys."

He grabbed her in a hard embrace. "I'm not ever leaving you in the middle of the night or any other time."

"I knew I'd picked the right man."

"Say," he asked with a soft chuckle. "What do you see in me, anyway?"

"Joy." Abigail patted his rear, her voice husky, "forever joy."

He scooped her up and carried her to the car he'd rented. "I have plenty of that, babe." His stride lengthened. "Enough to last for forever."

THE STETSON

THE END

WWW.PJWOMACK.COM

ABOUT THE AUTHOR

I have always loved books, reading a passion early in my life. I read everything the famous and not so famous authors wrote. I was a die hard historical romance only fan until I found contemporary to be just as satisfying to read. I began the rocky journey to publication blind to all the rules and terribly afraid of rejection. With the help of patient critique partners and surviving more than a few disappointments, my first full-length novel was accepted for publication.

I live in the Mid-West, and enjoy being near my two adult children and my wonderful wildflower garden. I will never stop being delighted by the notes sent by a reader commenting on my work. Hearing from readers is important to me. I want to write stories that stay with you for a long while. I do it all for you.

Siren Publishing, Inc.
www.SirenPublishing.com

CPSIA information can be obtained at www.ICGtesting.com
Printed in the USA
BVOW02s1140030114

340849BV00016B/427/P